Etha... ...y to her c... ...pt
to ste... that kiss he was aching for

He never had liked her mother's front stoop, a concrete block with two steps cut into it. There was nowhere to hide up there under the porch light. Grasping Kelsey's arm before she could take that first step, he firmly yanked her behind the closest azalea bush.

Kelsey gasped, her eyes dancing in the shadows. "What's all this? Are we doing the old hide-and-seek thing?"

"The adult version, where nobody hides." He cupped her chin and locked his mouth to hers for a bold, hot taste. She didn't resist at all.

The impossible dream was beginning to unfold. It just wasn't supposed to happen behind a bush. In the end it was the sound of his own car horn, in the care of the two teens, that brought Ethan back to his senses. "Guess this is good-night," he said, halfheartedly.

"Yes, Ethan." With a sweet smile she urged him out from behind the shrub. "Thanks a lot. I had so much fun."

The car horn honked again, making him scowl. "I better go." He backed away, pointing a finger at her. "To be continued."

Dear Reader,

The signpost ahead reads Maple Junction, Wisconsin.
You're arriving just in time to make the trip with
hometown girl Kelsey Graham. She's been away for
ten years and is very unsure what to expect, even
from trusty boy-next-door Ethan Taggert. Along the
path to maturity they'd played off one another in
fits of pleasure, frustration and disappointment,
never quite clicking to make a lasting love match.
Despite the fact that they'd parted on a note of
disappointment, Ethan is determined to finally make
that love connection happen.

Readers often wonder what inspires my writing. This
particular story originated with a brief article about
a prom couple's fatal accident along a rural road.
The idea that such a euphoric event could turn so
devastating deeply touched me. I quickly began to
formulate a story through a series of questions. What
if a passenger in the car survived? What if her small
town blamed her for the crash? What if a memory
loss prevented her from knowing the truth herself?
Could faith, forgiveness and a little detective work
finally make things better?

Kelsey soon came into being, followed by the boy
who'd loved her, lost her and lived to regret it. I hope
you enjoy the result.

Warm regards as always,

Leandra Logan

The Sheriff's Second Chance

LEANDRA LOGAN

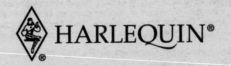

HARLEQUIN®

TORONTO • NEW YORK • LONDON
AMSTERDAM • PARIS • SYDNEY • HAMBURG
STOCKHOLM • ATHENS • TOKYO • MILAN • MADRID
PRAGUE • WARSAW • BUDAPEST • AUCKLAND

ISBN-13: 978-0-373-75156-3
ISBN-10:   0-373-75156-7

THE SHERIFF'S SECOND CHANCE

This edition published by arrangement with Harlequin Books S.A.

® and TM are trademarks of the publisher. Trademarks indicated with
® are registered in the United States Patent and Trademark Office, the
Canadian Trade Marks Office and in other countries.

www.eHarlequin.com

Printed in U.S.A.

ABOUT THE AUTHOR

Leandra Logan is an award-winning author with over thirty books to her credit. She lives in the historic Minnesota town of Stillwater with her husband. Her interests include boating, golfing, gardening and spending time with children and friends.

Books by Leandra Logan

HARLEQUIN AMERICAN ROMANCE

Chapter One

It was the end of another school year.

Kelsey Graham sat at her broad oak desk at the front of the classroom, sorting through the homemade cards and gifts from her twenty-three first graders. They were technically second graders now, which some of the cards made clear with large numeral twos carefully traced atop heads on stick bodies, and houses with small roofs and giant chimneys.

The seven-year-old mind, so full of imagination and hope, never ceased to fascinate and amaze her. Forget television. Give a kid some paper and a box of crayons....

It was easy for anyone to dream on such a beautiful day. To gaze beyond the long open windows facing the school courtyard, let the mind wander on the warm breezes scented with peonies and freshly cut grass.

Spring into summer plans! she'd quipped to her students this afternoon over homemade cookies and lemonade. Many of the youngsters had announced trips to Disney World, Cape Cod, Hawaii. No surprise in this affluent Philadelphia neighborhood.

The most important thing, she'd insisted, as they'd

crowded round for a farewell hug, was to enjoy their moms and dads, brothers and sisters. To laugh and play and tell stories, just as they had in the classroom. To take a few photographs to enjoy later on…

Kelsey's gaze landed back on the empty rows of pint-sized desks and she felt a wistful pang. Last Day Letdown. She recognized the symptoms very well, having suffered from them on this final day of each of the past five school years.

Fueled with new purpose, she gripped the edge of the desk, rolled back her chair and stood. She turned and began to dismantle the dancing alphabet display from one of the cork squares flanking the blackboard, dropping the colorful construction-paper pieces into a box on the floor. She'd need a ladder to get at the train of twelve boxcars, designating months of the year, tacked out of reach above the board.

As if by telepathy, janitor Marta Lynch appeared with a metal step ladder. Like Kelsey, she was trim and toned, of average height and weight. But Marta was a full decade older than Kelsey's twenty-eight years, and her clipped brown hair needed a routine dye job to cover some pesky gray strands. While Kelsey favored chic outfits like today's navy linen suit with pink nylon shell, peppy Marta wore casual clothing more suited to her job. Today's comical red T-shirt read Don't Wanna Work. A joke, indeed, as she never stopped.

"Hi, Kel," Marta chirped. "I figured you'd need your annual boost."

This was a pep talk to help Kelsey let go of yet another year's worth of bright faces that had shaped her life. In her own cheery way, Marta tried to steer Kelsey to activities that would make the summer months fly, and fill the void until another classful of kids marched in to give Kelsey's life fresh purpose and direction.

"Thanks, Marta," she said through a mouthful of stick pins.

"Hey, swallow those and you'll need an ambulance!" Marta propped the ladder against the wall to march over and pull the pins free.

There was an informality between Kelsey and all the maintenance staff that allowed this kind of scolding. She'd grown up working in her mother's Cozy Home Café back in tiny Maple Junction, Wisconsin where there were no prima donnas among the cooks, potato peelers and dishwashers in the kitchen. Everyone pitched in where needed without a whimper.

This democratic approach had not caught fire with most of the faculty here at Hancock Grammar School. The other teachers believed in keeping a lofty distance from the maintenance workers and felt it within their right to make pretentious demands of them. While Kelsey's friendlier approach wasn't a bid to score more perks, it did win her prompt spill cleanup and lightbulb replacements, as well as the latest hydraulic chair every autumn.

Marta had taken the pins to an open container on the desk and was perusing Kelsey's farewell loot.

"You can rummage," invited Kelsey. "I already noted who gave me what."

Marta chuckled as she picked up a shimmery pink sack of potpourri. "This is from the Walters boy. The principal has already put his in the trash." She moved the pin box to the chalk tray near the blackboard, looking Kelsey straight in the eye. "I advise you to do the same.

His granny uses some illegal substances along with the cinnamon and rosemary. Of the *hallucinatory kind*."

"Marta!" Kelsey laughed. "How ridiculous."

"Ha. Put that brew in your panty drawer and you risk being raided."

"It smells wonderful and will be fine in a bowl on my kitchen table." The table was just a small one that barely fit in the nook of her studio apartment, but she liked the word *kitchen*. She and her mother Clare both loved to cook.

Marta shrugged. "Well, at least don't set that nickel bag of tricks on fire."

"I think in today's market, the bags are worth at least a dime."

"Whatever." Marta strolled back to the desk and sifted through the cards, still heavy and damp with paste. "The sentiments on these are always so sweet—wishes and kisses, hearts and smiles."

"Yeah." Kelsey sighed and tugged at the crepe paper trimming the cork's wood frame. "So many big dreams in those little people. Unspoiled." For now.

"So, you and the boyfriend have any hot summer plans?"

"Tanner and I are finished."

"Really? For good?"

"You had to see it coming, Marta."

"I knew you weren't happy, but didn't know for sure he would be for the chop. After all, you've bickered before and had the best of fun making up."

Kelsey winced. "*The chop* sounds so brutal. We just said goodbye." Despite Marta's graphic terminology, there was no denying that she'd gotten the gist of Kelsey's relationship with Tanner. They shared a chemistry that kept them both hungry and satisfied, breaking up and making up.

Ultimately, she had been forced to face the reality that was Tanner. A bit younger than Kelsey, he was still wangling the best deal his communications degree could get him. During this quest, he worked at Starbucks, obsessed over basketball and video games. There were also Tanner's parties. Much like fraternity bashes, they centered around junk food and a keg of beer. Understandable, perhaps, as Tanner had only been out of college two years.

Kelsey had foolishly decided to hurry along his maturity, offering direction and fresh goals. After all, he had so much potential. But in the heat of their worst argument ever, he'd accused her of treating him like one of her students.

Tanner had Kelsey figured and had every right to be annoyed. Of course, he was clueless why she'd suddenly changed. Kelsey had originally been attracted to his aimless approach because her own college years had been pretty grim, dealing with regrets better left back in Maple Junction.

Sadly, she'd finally discovered it was too late for a replay.

She could have loosened up a bit more, got into hip-hop and learned to navigate a PlayStation. But she didn't really want to.

"On second thought, maybe there is no better way to describe my breakup than *the chop.*"

Rather than amuse Marta, this remark deepened her frown. "Maybe you should've hung on to him through the summer, just for some fun."

"No. I can't bear one more burping rendition of the

Green Acres theme song from a gang of magna-cum-laude grads." Kelsey tossed the last of the colorful display into the box and joined Marta at the desk.

"How will you fill your time?" Marta asked bleakly.

"Well, there's Toby Schuler and Debbie Kinny, they seem friendly," said Kelsey, referring to two singles who'd joined the teaching staff that year.

"Oh, sure. Toby is a mama's boy who's going to spend the summer watching movies. As for Debbie, all she plans to do is haunt the thrift stores and read trashy magazines." At Kelsey's look of surprise, Marta shrugged. "I hear loads of stuff cleaning the faculty lounge. People act like I'm not even there and it's a mighty handy way to get a scoop."

"Okay, so I save them for an emergency. I also have my girlfriends from college."

"Every year, more of those Bryn Mawr College pals are getting married and moving to the suburbs."

"They're not exactly dead yet," Kelsey grumbled.

"Death and marriage are similar transitions in the eye of a single person, right? I mean, when it comes down to availability."

With a huff, Kelsey set her briefcase atop the clutter, released the twin clasps and opened the lid. "Make yourself useful and help me stack the cards in here."

Marta admired a card cut into a crooked half moon before putting it in the case. "You know what I mean. When you're single there's always a hassle in getting together with married girlfriends. The hubby's brother is coming to dinner, or the baby has a diaper rash, or the older kid has a tuba lesson."

Kelsey eyed her wryly. "Those some of your excuses to friends?"

"I only wish my boys had played an instrument. But as you know, they only love hockey. As it turns out, most of my friends are the mothers of other players. I guess it's because we spend so much time together in the bleachers. You're welcome to hang out with me—" she paused "—in a pinch."

"I don't think I'd fit in without my own hockey player." Kelsey left the greeting cards to Marta and retrieved an empty baked bean box from the floor to pack away the gifts. "Stop worrying. I'll be fine."

Marta picked up a bottle of cheap cologne, popped the cap and took a whiff. "Phew! Lily of the valley. All the rage over at the nursing home."

Kelsey snatched it away and set it gently in the box. "Do the cards." She'd collected a pretty wooden birdhouse she could put on her condo's small balcony, a box of chocolates for her nightstand and a collection of colored ink pens she'd use to write letters to her mother. Clare wasn't into e-mails or anything to do with computers for that matter. She wasn't open to change, being entirely focused on the café. Just as Kelsey was with teaching.

Among the wealth of gifts, there were a number of mugs proclaiming her World's Best Teacher. Even with a cupboard full of them, she still enjoyed getting more, as each one was reinforcement of her life's narrow mission.

Moving the briefcase to the opposite side of the desk, Marta tipped it just enough to send the contents sliding and expose some of the personal papers Kelsey routinely dealt with during her free time.

Marta spouted, "No harm done," before righting the case again but suddenly spotted a neon-orange sheet of paper. "Hey, what's this?"

"Nothing." Kelsey tried to grab it, but Marta was

too quick for her. With a deft move likely learned from a hockey son, she ducked and spun on worn Nike running shoes. Caught on spike-heeled pumps, Kelsey was no match.

"Reunion," Marta said, skimming the sheet with interest. "Class of ninety-seven. This is about your tenth high-school reunion in Maple Junction!"

"Yes, but—"

"Empty months ahead and you never said a word about this opportunity."

Kelsey flapped her hands. "Stop! I'm not interested."

Marta ignored her. "Two weeks away. You've got plenty of time to get some new outfits, a haircut."

"Dammit, Marta, I am not going," Kelsey insisted. "I've closed the door on that part of my life."

"But you've got some nice childhood memories."

She folded her arms defensively. "I know."

"It'll be a good change for you, especially after dumping Tanner."

"I have my summer all mapped out," Kelsey protested. "Days of reading books on the beach, jogging, whacking golf balls at the driving range. Nights downtown seeing plays, eating formal dinners served by polite waiters and drinking cocktails mixed by cocky bartenders."

"By yourself!"

"Probably. Mostly. I'm fine with it, so let's drop the whole issue."

"Whatever." Marta went over to retrieve her ladder, tipping it against the strip of cork over the blackboard where the paper train was.

"I can climb that thing," Kelsey said.

"Not in those heels, you can't. It would be as dangerous as putting pins in your mouth." Taking the rungs with ease, Marta looked down on her distracted friend, now engrossed in the flyer. "Opportunity is knockin'…"

"Marta, please!"

"Just seems high time to take another look at that hometown situation."

"Three of my good friends died, along with all their big dreams for the future. That's more than a situation, it's nothing short of a tragedy."

"It's more of a tragedy if your dreams died, too."

Kelsey hung her head. "Well, maybe I deserve it."

"You've been punishing yourself for ten years," Marta said gently. "That seems a stiff penalty for an unintentional spinout on a dark rainy road. Besides, you aren't absolutely sure you were even driving."

The awful accident had indeed resulted in a head injury that robbed Kelsey of any memory of that night's prom festivities, including details of the crash itself. However, since she was found near the driver's door of the Jetta, and had later admitted her inexperience in handling a stick shift, the police had deduced that she'd likely been the fumbler behind the wheel.

Kelsey had been far too spunky back then to accept full responsibility for an event she couldn't even remember, especially as it could have resulted in a manslaughter charge. Just the same, her heart remained broken, regret and remorse gnawing at the wound.

In a way, she understood the public's initial mistrustful outcry. She had had a reputation for daring deeds—daring for Maple Junction anyway—like scaling high fences, skiing down perilous roads closed during the winter's iciest weeks, somersaulting off the high board at the community swimming pool. And there was never any question that she would top Whittier High's cheerleader pyramid during any given routine.

While scarcely a pattern of seriously reckless behavior, it hadn't helped her case. For most people, it proved to be a small leap in judgment to assume she had climbed behind the wheel of her boyfriend Brad's car and driven under those dangerous conditions.

The controversy remained unresolved to this day. Without solid proof of her guilt, the cops were stalled and she in turn could raise no tangible defense.

"If you'd seemed content here all these years, I wouldn't be pressing the issue," Marta broke in gently. "But it's plain to see you've been settling for a fairly narrow life with just a handful of relationships. Forgive me if I'm being too pushy, but for the first time since we've met, you seem primed to move forward. You dumped the Boy Wonder and hung on to that flyer for a reason! Maybe you want to go home more than you realize."

"People wanted me gone quite badly back then. In fact they shunned me. I wouldn't know where to begin with them."

"Simply be yourself, who's a wonderful person, I might add. You're as sorry as anybody about what happened," Marta speculated. "That should count for something."

"Brad's folks, Lewis and Bailey Cutler, are bound to be sorrier for a start. Their life revolved around their only son."

"They are likely still feeling the pain more than most, but I'm confident you can win them over. You did the first time around."

An image of Brad popped into her head. His striking white-blond hair, clear blue eyes, well-proportioned features and the brilliant smile that had made him all the more handsome. He'd been smiling big the day he'd first taken Kelsey home to the Cutler estate to meet his parents. The son of the richest, most powerful man in town, determined to date the middle-class café owner's daughter. She smiled faintly. They'd taken the trouble to get to know her because they'd respected Brad's opinion and he'd so badly wanted them to approve of her.

"It all fell into place like a dream," she admitted. "We got on great and they began to look forward to me being part of the family one day. It was going to be fantastic, Marta." Her smile faded. "But it's all gone. The magic died with Brad."

"That old magic, yes. But the world hums with a new magic each and every day, even back in Maple Junction. It's high time you checked it out and decided once and for all where you belong."

"What if going back makes me feel even worse?"

"At least you'll know you tried. In any case, it's bound to help you move on." Marta descended the ladder to stand at her elbow, her excitement growing. "So have you bounced the idea off your mother yet?"

"Uh, no."

"Well, you should. She for one will be thrilled to see you."

This wasn't necessarily true. Marta had met Clare Graham several times when she'd visited Philadelphia. But Marta didn't understand that the cordial vacationer was vastly different from the sober café owner. Like Kelsey, Clare was burdened with a heavy guilt over the car crash. No wonder, as folks simmering with grief and rage had suddenly branded her a bad parent for raising such a reckless daughter, and initially had punished her by avoiding the café. Clare had long insisted business was fine again, and Kelsey had taken her at her word.

Just the same, Clare had never once coaxed her to come back and had never offered a mother's absolution for what had happened. This hurt Kelsey but she struggled to be realistic. How could she expect her mother to be stronger than herself? Kelsey never broached the idea of returning either. And when they did on rare occasions speak of the accident, they still fed off each other's guilt. Having lost Kelsey's father, Paul, to a brain aneurism when Kelsey was nearly ten, they both fully understood the gaping hole that death left in a family.

On the other hand, they'd always been a team because of his death, keeping the café up and running together. Kelsey missed the close bond they'd once shared and wanted it back.

Later that evening, back at her dinky downtown condo on Monroe Avenue, Kelsey sat at the table in her nook with her new set of colored pens and an assortment of stationery. Also in front of her was the acceptance form from the reunion flyer, filled out and clipped along the dotted line.

With a flourish she stuffed the form, a cheery note and a check for the fifty-dollar fee into an envelope addressed to the reunion coordinator, her closest childhood friend, Sarah Yates. Done! No turning back now. She was homeward bound.

Marta's efforts had given her the final nudge she'd needed. The past decade in Philadelphia had indeed been a disappointment, nothing like her original dreams of teaching alongside Sarah at the local elementary school, then marriage and kids. Her inability to rise above those old hometown hurts had kept her emotionally frozen.

Perhaps the only way to move forward was to first take the trip back.

On many levels the very idea was scary, preposterous. Would *anyone* welcome her? To make this work, she had to believe they would. That even if they couldn't forget what had happened, they'd be willing to forgive.

Then with any luck, maybe she could finally forgive herself.

She needed to let her mother know. Although it seemed most reasonable just to call, Kelsey knew that if she detected the tiniest bit of hesitation in Clare's tone, she'd chicken out.

Picking up a pen with cheery orange ink, she held it over some bright floral-bordered paper, rehearsing aloud what she'd write.

"Dear Mom. It's been awhile since you've visited Pennsylvania. Too long, really. Seems about time I came back to Wisconsin.

"Dear Mom, Guess what? Wonderful news. I'm coming home."

With a sigh, she set pen to paper. "Dear Mom, Just want to prepare you. I'm returning home for the reunion…."

Chapter Two

Sheriff Ethan Taggert was still at the station when the emergency call came in from the Cutler mansion, so he responded in the squad car. With siren blaring and roof bar lights flashing, he tore down Cutler Trail doing close to eighty.

The trail had been named 150 years ago, when Thomas Cutler had bought a thousand acres along what had amounted to a bumpy narrow ditch. He'd built a house, made the ditch a road and started up a newspaper. The newspaper was the start of an empire that had soon grown to include several local businesses, including the bank, and had made the family a fortune.

Thomas Cutler had wasted no time advertising far and wide that Maple Junction, Wisconsin, was a quaint dairy town worth visiting by horseless carriage. There was toboggan racing in the winter, maple-syrup tapping in the spring, strawberry picking in the summer, and the corn harvest in the autumn, and each had spawned its own festival, not to mention a county fair and several horse shows.

And all were reported in the daily paper, the *Cutler Express*.

All looked quiet as Ethan wheeled through the estate's huge steel gates and up the sweeping paved drive. The windows of the sprawling stone mansion were alight, glowing on all three levels.

He desperately hoped Lewis hadn't had another heart attack….

Lewis had become a second father to Ethan ever since, as four-year-olds, he and Lewis's son Bradley had enjoyed a weekly wrestle under the willow trees outside church each Sunday. With parents too busy with chores and errands, young kids in the small rural community didn't get to play together too often, so he'd started to really look forward to Sundays.

In due time, after Ethan had mastered tying his own shoes, his mother had started to drop him off at the mansion for play dates. The boys had spent their time kicking a soccer ball, digging holes in search of treasure and wading through swampland to catch toads, all fuelled by piles of sandwiches.

Ethan's bond with the Cutlers had only strengthened with time. Ethan's dad traveled selling insurance, so it was Lewis who'd supported the boys at school, taken them to professional sporting events and had been on hand for nearly every milestone in their lives. Lewis had loved to push envelopes and pull strings for them. Some of that push-pull still went on. While Ethan was more than confident in his role as sheriff, it was Lewis who'd helped swing his election last year.

A uniformed maid pulled open the heavy front door before Ethan could get his hand around the brass handle. It was the eldest Parker daughter, Carol, who'd dropped out of UW–Madison in midterm to rethink her future. Ethan had dated her on occasion and had found her a bit boring. Just the same, he hoped they would always be friends. She was just the friend he needed tonight. Carol had been working for the Cutlers for four months and knew enough about household politics to clue him in.

"Faster than a speeding bullet tonight, aren't ya?" she greeted coyly.

Brushing by her, Ethan hurried into the dim cavernous foyer, glancing up the wide staircase. "Where is he, Carol? Up with the doc?"

"Nope. Right in there." She calmly tipped her curly orange head left, toward the study.

"Did he collapse? What happened?"

Carol reached to stroke some short brown strands of hair from his forehead in a gesture he thought far too intimate. "I'm not sure."

He gave her shoulders a mild shake, hoping to rattle her composure. "Did anybody call an ambulance?"

Slowly and with a mysterious smile that seemed to suggest she was enjoying his touch, she replied, "Nobody else was called. You're all he wants."

Confused, Ethan strode off through the walnut door into the spacious den he knew was Lewis Cutler's comfort room. It was where he came to plot, relax, dream. And brood. Ethan suspected the latter was true tonight as he found Lewis seated in his favorite leather recliner, accepting a snifter of brandy from his wife, Bailey. Judging by the filmy glass and Cutler's equally filmy eyes, it was likely a refill.

"Finally, Ethan!"

Ethan was a bit startled to discover a fully functioning Lewis. Carol's lack of urgency was suddenly more understandable. "What exactly is the matter here, Lew?"

Lewis leaned forward in his chair. "Have you heard?"

"Heard what?"

"The news. The horrible news."

Ethan appealed to Bailey. In her blue satin lounging pajamas, a paperback and eyeglasses clutched in one hand, she appeared to have been abruptly summoned, too. Now, unseen by Lewis, whose blood pressure could stand nothing but her utter faith and devotion, she stared off into space with strained patience.

"Leave us, Bailey," Lewis directed, a bit more gently. "You needn't be concerned with this."

Bailey hated the dismissal. She frowned and opened her mouth, but then as was expected, closed it again. Holding herself like a model, she exited obediently and Ethan was struck, not for the first time, how beautiful the fiftyish platinum blonde was. Their son Brad had favored her and had been truly grateful for it.

"So what is this news, Lew?" Ethan demanded.

Lewis wheezed—courtesy of his cigar smoking— then swigged down another slug of brandy. "Kelsey Graham. Returning for your class reunion."

"Really." Ethan's heart jumped wildly in his chest. He worked to keep his voice even. "Still, might be just a rumor."

"I made a few calls. Trust me, it's true."

Ethan didn't think to doubt the sharp newspaper mogul's sources.

Lewis glared into the flames flickering in the old marble fireplace. It wasn't a particularly cold June evening, but there was a slight chill in the air since a thundershower that afternoon. Lewis felt the cold more easily these days, deep in his bones where brandy couldn't seep. He was a baker's dozen years older than his wife and the gap seemed more pronounced than ever. Ethan knew Lewis regretted not diving into marriage sooner, like he had everything else, and having a bundle of kids. His late start had produced only one son. And Brad's life had been so tragically short.

"How dare she come back?" Lewis thundered. "The girl who killed our Brad." He rested drunken eyes on Ethan, eyes which looked moist.

Raw emotion swelled inside Ethan threatening to leave him splintered and miserable. He tamped it down with remarkable control. "Whatever happened out there on Route 6 that night, Lew—" he struggled for his voice "—was an accident."

"She killed my precious boy." Big tears of despair began to spill.

Ethan had the sudden urge to bolt, to escape a replay of the decade-old mess. But he was dealt in permanently at the Cutler's table, as intimately as he had been back in his frog-catching days. With his own parents relocated to Arizona, Ethan most often turned to Lewis for financial advice, fishing company, or just to rehash a ball game.

Staying numb was his only chance. He abruptly strode across to the room's wet bar and poured himself a short whiskey. The brandy Lewis was guzzling cost three hundred bucks a bottle and, in Ethan's opinion, was stuff to be saved strictly for the good times.

Ethan wandered round the big room sipping his drink, taking in the sameness, the security he'd always felt here. A stuffed moose head, trophies for shooting, a mantel full of photos of Ethan and Brad growing up. Lewis loved showing off his wide range of skills, as hunter, mogul and mentor. When the boys were in high school, the room had featured pictures of Kelsey as well. For two and a half years she'd been a valued part of this family, just like Ethan.

Kelsey Graham, the love of Bradley Cutler's young life. Who'd apparently smashed up his sporty black VW Jetta on prom night, killing not only Brad, but friends Todd Marshall and Lissa Hanson.

"I had an agreement with the mother," Lewis muttered. "Ship Kelsey off to Bryn Mawr and I would put a stop to any town boycott of her café."

Ethan arched a brow. "Was there a boycott in the works?"

"The way everyone loved those three dead kids? Who'd support a restaurant harboring her?"

"But sending her to Philadelphia seemed so extreme, when she was already enrolled at the University of Wisconsin like the rest of us."

"Had she gone to school in Madison with you, she could've commuted back here on weekends. Like nothing ever happened. Intolerable."

This was the first Ethan had heard of any embargo on the café. But the town had been hysterical back then. The only thing folks seemed to agree on was the basic account of the accident: Kelsey had lost control on a dark slick curve out in the countryside and had hit a tree, ejecting all four kids on impact. Brad and Lissa had died at the scene. Kelsey and Todd had been raced to Maple County Hospital for treatment, where Todd had died without regaining consciousness.

Ethan shook off a shiver as he recalled how he'd gone to the prom in the Jetta. But his date had gotten ill halfway through the evening and he'd taken her home by taxi. He'd returned to the party to discover Brad and Kelsey had left with Todd and Lissa. Understandable, as he wouldn't have been any fun solo. While it had been a disappointment at the time, Susie Moore's flu bug had probably saved both their lives.

"I can't help but wonder how she found out about the reunion in the first place," Lewis grumbled.

"She probably was sent an invitation along with the rest of us."

"Who'd do that!"

"Does that really matter?" Ethan asked quietly.

"Yes. I'd like to know who was so careless, who didn't even think to consult me first."

The self-appointed town leader would expect to be shown such deference. Over the years people had helped fuel his huge ego by catering to him even as they accepted his advice and help in all sorts of civic and business matters. He'd always been extremely generous with his time and money, as long as no one challenged his autocratic streak. Lewis's biggest weakness was his habit of holding grudges.

"Derek's wife was her best friend…." Lewis scowled. "But she wouldn't dare. Not after all I've done for Derek."

Of course she'd dare! Ethan pressed his lips firmly to conceal a smile. Sarah Yates never deferred to her husband and had always stayed close with Kelsey. Small tidbits about Kelsey slipped out of her on occasion, confirming they were still in touch.

Ethan landed in a beige club chair near Lewis's, regarding him with concern. "This stress can't be good for you, Lew. You already had that one heart attack."

The aged and fleshy chin lifted. "It was just a flutter."

That wasn't true at all. It had been fairly serious, and he had been hospitalized for several days while they'd run tests. "Whatever you call it, you're not supposed to get too riled."

This attempt at reason seemed to bounce off Lewis's granite features, still trained on the fire. "Pity those old manslaughter charges didn't stick. I sure wish there was a way of charging that girl now."

The very idea made Ethan sick to his stomach. "There wasn't enough evidence then, so it would be even harder today."

"When I think how my critically injured boy managed to crawl round the car to reach her. It surely hastened his death. If only he'd stayed put. If only I'd gotten help there in time."

It was that murky issue of time that had Ethan running the siren tonight. Just in case another Cutler life hung on a matter of minutes. But whatever Brad had done on his own in the end, it had been his choice, not Kelsey's.

Lewis ponderously sipped some brandy. "Wonder what she wants. Exactly…"

Seemed obvious to Ethan. "To see her mother, I should think."

"Do you really believe it's that simple?"

"Yes…" Ethan's voice trailed off as he stared at Lewis, wondering if there was something significant behind his wizened look. But what could it be? "I seriously doubt Kelsey has an ulterior motive," he said more strongly. "She and Clare must miss each other terribly.

A family of two, unless you count Clare's brother, Teddy."

"Who's never counted for much," Lewis grunted.

"There's not a more gentle woman in town than Clare Graham. Their separation has to be painful, all those holidays apart."

"At least when Clare talks to Kelsey, she gets an answer. No long-distance line has yet been invented to connect me with Brad."

Ethan lowered his head. "I know you miss him. I do, too. I've tried my best to be there for you—in his place."

"Of course you have. Why the minute I sized you up years back in that cheap Sunday suit, with a crummy haircut and first-class brain, I knew you were special. You're the spare son Bailey and I longed for and you've never let us down once," he assured. "However, that has nothing to do with my ongoing issue with the Grahams."

"But it does for two obvious reasons. In my role as sheriff, it's my duty to serve all citizens of Maple Junction equally, including the Grahams. And as a former next-door neighbor to the family, I'm fond of Clare. I know I'm asking a big favor, but I think it would be in everyone's best interest for you to soft pedal your reaction to Kelsey's visit."

"Huh. I'm entitled to my opinion!"

"But your opinions carry so much more weight than most," Ethan reasoned. "People will follow your lead on this without giving Kelsey a fair chance."

"Now you're saying I'm being unfair to her?"

"We haven't discussed this situation in quite some time and I must admit I'm a bit surprised at how strong your ill feelings still are."

"Well, I'm entitled. Give it some deeper thought."

"I was going to suggest the same thing to you." Ethan rose, went to set his empty glass back on the wet bar. "Guess I'll be going. Try and get some rest."

Lewis watched him anxiously. "How can I sleep without knowing what the Graham girl is really up to?"

Squaring his tense shoulders, Ethan turned back to him. "Trust me, it's *nothing*."

"She must have an agenda," he persisted. "Everybody does. Do me a favor and dig into it a little."

"What am I looking for?"

"Find out who invited her and when exactly she's due back. Call everyone on that reunion committee if you have to."

Ethan realized he wanted to know those things himself. A word with Sarah Yates would be sufficient. "All right, Lew. I'll check into it and get back to you."

"I'll be waiting by the phone."

"Tonight?"

"Yes."

"Gee, got any other whims that need immediate humoring?"

Lewis held out his empty glass to Ethan for another slug of brandy.

"SARAH! DON'T MOVE."

"But I heard a car door slam."

"I know. It's Ethan."

"So what?"

"Whisper, Sarah. Whisper."

"So what?" she repeated under her breath.

Sarah watched her husband, Derek, ease into their bedroom and flatten his body against the closed door.

He looked ridiculous. Sarah was curled up in a rocker near the crib. Watching the infant sleep by the light of the moon was Sarah's favorite new pastime.

Derek wiped his forehead. "Whew! I closed the windows just in time."

"In time for what?"

"To muffle Amy Joy's cry. If she cries."

"Oh, she's gonna cry, the way he's started to lean on that doorbell."

Right on cue, Amy Joy twisted in her crib and let out a squeaky wail.

Derek abandoned his post at the door, snatched the baby off the little mattress and popped her into Sarah's arms. "Feed her, honey."

"She isn't hungry, just mad that she has a crazy dad."

"She can't suspect that at two months old."

"She already knows it at only seven weeks."

"This isn't funny. Please quiet her, Sare!"

With a gentle Madonna smile, Sarah tossed a hank of gold hair over her shoulder, opened her shirt and bra, and settled the baby in a suckling position at her breast. "Why are we acting like secret agents, and stupid ones at that?"

Derek's eyes darted nervously in the shadows. "Because Ethan's gotta be here about Kelsey."

"You can't be sure."

"Oh no? The news about her coming home got out today. And since Amy Joy arrived, nobody generally bugs us this late anymore."

"Is that all you have to go on?"

"My instincts tell me I'm right."

Sarah wasn't about to argue with his instincts. Born on the wrong side of the tracks to an abusive father and an overworked mother, Derek had been on the loose early, often one step ahead of the law due to the home-made rattletrap motorcycle he'd ridden without a license. For all intents and purposes, Derek was now a new man. Except for that lingering sense of smell that never failed to pick up trouble.

Derek's features hardened. "He's just gotta be here on behalf of a very hot Lewis, to get hard answers for the old coot."

"About who to blame for Kelsey's return?" she surmised.

"Bingo. He's stopped ringing the bell...." He opened the bedroom door and stepped into the hallway. Then shut himself back in again with a soft oath. "He's still out there. Waiting."

"Ethan is too obliging to that old tyrant," Sarah complained.

"Sure he is. But when it comes down to it, we can't afford to anger Lewis either. He holds the title to my garage and has funneled so many regular customers my way." Derek raked a hand through his shaggy black hair. "I can't wait to own that place free and clear."

It would be awhile yet, Sarah knew, even with her teaching kindergarten. "Maybe we should've waited to start a family."

"No, honey, no. We waited long enough. Too long."

A faint rap now replaced the ringing bell. She sighed, hoisting the baby onto her shoulder to pat out a burp. "I'm not sure we're gaining anything by hiding like this."

"We're gaining time. Time for Lewis to settle down. Time for us to figure a logical reason for luring Kelsey back." Derek dropped to one knee beside the rocker. Despite his miffed tone, there was no mistaking the adoring look he bestowed on his girls.

"I suppose I may have acted rashly, sending Kelsey that flyer without even telling you."

He widened his eyes. "*May* have?"

"We do discuss important things first as a rule. But I can't—won't try to excuse this away with logic. I simply love her. She's the best friend I ever had—ever could have. Too much time has already been wasted while we miss out on all the dreams we had together as children. If only I could go back and change the day she left on that Greyhound."

"And do what?" Derek asked gently.

She rubbed her husband's stubbled cheek, inhaling the smell of motor oil that always clung to him before a shower. There was no answer, of course. Any healing course of action had been up to the adults. Instead they'd chosen to railroad an eighteen-year-old girl.

"All that matters now is that I want her back. I need her back."

"It's only a class reunion, hon."

"Maybe."

"Sarah…" Derek sounded almost afraid then.

"She might stay. With some encouragement."

He touched his baby's downy head. "Please don't expect too much. People change."

"Funny, I was thinking how some things never change. How people hold grudges, never give second chances."

"Sums up our man Cutler, all right. But please, don't rile him too much."

"He is being unreasonable."

"He did lose his kid, Sarah." He squeezed their baby's tiny foot. "Something we've come to understand so much better in the past seven weeks."

"Ah, there goes Ethan," Sarah said suddenly, gazing

out the side window just as the taillights of the squad car winked red on the street.

Derek took the sleeping baby and set her back in the crib. Then he put loving hands on his wife. "Come to bed with me."

Her mouth curved. "You know Doc says we should wait another week before we have sex, because of all my stitches."

He lifted her in his arms anyway, his voice growing husky. "I just want to hold you for a while. In the moonlight…"

Sarah understood. Sometimes, the town's insecure ex-bad boy needed a reminder that she was totally his.

Spooned into him on the broad mattress, she was not surprised when his soft snores told her he'd drifted off. He'd been working extra hours at the garage lately with his lone employee, Richard, in an effort to be the big breadwinner, to give her the stay-at-home-mom option next autumn. It was silly, really. She had no qualms about leaving Amy Joy with her mother, Isabel, for a few hours each day while she went to work. Derek's problem was that he'd watched his own mother drive herself into a frazzle in order to make ends meet. Their situation was nothing like that. She loved her job. It was the perfect part-time career, half days with summers off.

The conflict of interest with Lewis Cutler over Kelsey, however, was a far more troubling issue. It was bound to affect Ethan and Derek, who both enjoyed being close to the powerful man, but who also had connections to Kelsey.

It had all started for Ethan much earlier, invited through the Cutler front door as a toddler by Brad. Such an arrangement had been unthinkable for Derek back then, as his mother, Linda, had actually been a domestic at the class-conscious mansion. Derek hadn't made the Cutler connection until years later on the high school's prom night. Too poor to attend the prom himself, and not yet in Sarah's romantic sights, Derek had spent the evening roaring round the countryside on his motorcycle. He'd happened upon Brad's smashed Jetta, surveyed the casualties and raced over to the estate to alert Lewis. Even then he'd circled to the back door of the mansion.

Because of Derek, Lewis had managed a last word with his dying son. Suddenly, the class rebel, long taunted by the likes of Brad and so many others, had been in Lewis's good graces. Lewis had shed a new positive light on Derek along Harvester Avenue, had referred to him as a spirited and scrappy lad who, Lewis had discovered, was a whiz at fixing stuff like toasters, lamps, radios and motorbikes—especially motorbikes. He'd got Derek a room in the widow Watson's boardinghouse, had eventually arranged for Derek to buy the town's only auto-repair shop from a retiring Mel Trumbull, using his position as officer at the bank to float Derek a very low-interest loan.

Another Maple Junction happy ending courtesy of fairy godfather Lewis, who'd turned the lone rebel into a respected car mechanic, simultaneously repaying the boy's good deed and filling a vital job vacancy.

Sarah had eventually taken notice of Derek's turn-around while home from UW–Madison one weekend. She'd gotten a flat tire on the way into town one Friday night and had called Maple's only full-service garage. He'd fixed the tire and thrown in a tune-up. She'd taken him to lunch. After that, the favors had kept on flying. He'd changed her oil. She'd helped him shop for clothes. He'd fixed her parents' leaky sink. She'd taken him to movies with more dialogue than explosions.

When she graduated, he'd presented her with a modest engagement ring. A no-frills elopement had soon followed, as had the purchase of their house, made possible by her unspent wedding fund and a generous gift from the Cutlers.

Sarah sighed against her pillow. Everything had been going so well for so long. But only because nobody ever crossed Lewis Cutler. She wouldn't usually be doing it herself. But this was for Kelsey. Who, just like the rest of them, had a legitimate birthright here in Maple Junction.

Chapter Three

Ethan was edgy at the sheriff's office the next morning, determined to track down Sarah for a quick, frank talk about Kelsey. Why hadn't she answered the door last night? It would have been easy to find her two weeks ago when school was still in session. Despite the arrival of Amy Joy, Sarah had watched over her morning kindergarten class most days, relying on her aide to handle the get-up-and-go tasks. Occasionally, the baby had even hitched a ride along in her buggy. Things were like that in the small town, with obliging parents and staff wanting to make it easy for Sarah so she'd return next year.

It turned out all Ethan had to do was hit Harvester Avenue, where he spotted willowy Sarah sitting idle on a bench in front of the corner drugstore at Fifth Street, her hand gently rocking Amy Joy's big springy buggy.

Pretty as a picture was the new mother, dressed in a green peasant blouse and denim shorts, her wavy gold hair captured in a ribbon. With bare legs crossed, she bobbed a sandaled foot in time to "Spanish Flea," an Herb Alpert tune played by two clarinetists from the Whittier High School band busking at the corner.

Amused passersby were tossing coins into an upside-down baseball cap.

The boys froze at the sight of him, probably wondering if they needed a permit to play.

Ethan didn't know or care. "Go ahead, knock yourselves out."

Happy, they tooted on with gusto.

Peeking at the dozing baby under the buggy's visor, Ethan leaned against a nearby lamppost. Sarah wasn't going to be able to avoid him this time. Funny that she'd tried it last night. But she was one tough girl and had kicked him out of the treehouse in her father's apple orchard more than once. Landing on apples sure did hurt! He still couldn't bear to eat one.

"Nice day, Sarah," he greeted genially.

"Perfect."

"How's our baby girl doing?"

"Swell. As you can see for yourself."

"They grow up so fast," he marveled. "Assert their independence so early."

She gaped at him. "What do you mean?"

"I could've sworn I heard her crying alone in your house last night. Naturally, I got right off the bell. Waited though, to give her a sporting chance to respond but I guess she just couldn't crawl the distance."

"Don't be silly, Ethan."

"Of course if you had been there, you'd have answered the bell, right?"

"Well, sure. I mean, none of us were there. Must have been the radio you heard. Derek keeps it on when we go out. To fool burglars."

Her brown eyes were bright and steady in spite of the lie. She and Kelsey could sell anything to anyone back in the day—watered-down lemonade, bruised apples, day-old pastries, all with convincing sincerity. He expected that would still hold true, at least for her.

"So why did you drop by last night, Ethan?"

It was a smart move to ask, knowing she was already trapped.

"I was following up a rumor about Kelsey coming. Is it true?"

"Yes!" She clasped her hands gleefully. "A crazy twist, huh?"

The craziest.

"C'mon, take another look at Amy Joy," Sarah urged suddenly.

"Why?"

"This time, note the sweet little rosebud dress she's wearing."

He leaned back over the pram. "Very nice."

"Sent to her by guess who?"

"Kelsey."

"Exactly." She closed her eyes and smiled up at the sun. "Amy Joy's only outfit from out of town. Makes her look sharp and unique, like her aunt Kelsey."

It was becoming impossible to talk over the music. Ethan turned to discover there were now four musicians on the corner. He decided to sit on the bench beside Sarah to make himself heard. "How long have you known about Kelsey's homecoming?"

"I've kept the news under wraps a little while," she admitted. "There seemed no hurry in giving grudge-toting people time to get worked up about it and plan a negative campaign. So how is Mr. Grudge himself taking it?"

"Lewis is a little worked up."

"As expected."

"Is he the reason you pretended not to be home last night, Sare?"

"Okay, yes," she relented. "Neither Derek or I felt like dealing with the Cutler issue at that hour."

"He's bound to have an interest, Sarah. In his mind, Kelsey robbed him of his only child, his main reason for living."

Sarah's face hardened suddenly. "You know as well as I do that Kelsey didn't hurt anyone on purpose. Ever."

"Still, the fact remains—"

"Cutler and those other fools drove the poor girl right out of town."

"A college education from Bryn Mawr is hardly a sentence at San Quentin."

"Oh, but how she struggled to earn it. She had to maintain the best grades to keep scholarships and worked some very crummy jobs."

"I guess I never realized."

"Nobody did. Kelsey was forced to take the fall for the accident, then it was out of sight, out of mind."

"Are you suggesting the case was poorly handled?"

"Sheriff Norton hardly solved it."

"He couldn't with so little to go on."

"I was highly suspicious of his methods even then."

"What I remember most is struggling with the loss. In the long run, it's all been about moving on, trying to forget."

Hoping to regain his composure, Ethan stood, dipped into his blue uniform shirt pocket for his sunglasses and put them on his lean, taut face. But Sarah wasn't finished with him.

"Maybe it's time we took a fresh look at the whole

mess, put a stop to the anger—encourage Kelsey to move home for good! That's exactly what I intend to do. Go stuff that in one of Lewis's big stinky hand-rolled cigars."

Encourage Kelsey to move home? That was what was behind this? Ethan was completely floored. The idea of having her back in town, so full of fun and wit, was one he'd given up on long ago.

Just then a big motor coach wheezed to a stop at the curb, the way it did every day round this time. Sarah signaled the band of musicians on the corner and they broke into the Whittier High anthem.

Suddenly things all fell into place in the gray matter behind the tinted lenses. Sarah wasn't out here by chance. Kelsey was due home the same way she'd left, on a Greyhound bus. This Greyhound bus.

Ethan inhaled sharply in anticipation as the bus door folded open.

Passengers disembarked, mostly a stream of UW students home for the summer.

He sensed Sarah standing beside him now, holding her breath, too.

The sliding door remained open but no one else appeared. False alarm maybe. It did seem impossible that after all these years Kelsey Graham was going to walk off this bus or any other bus to ever set foot back in Maple Junction.

Then a figure in a tight, colorfully striped sundress registered in his brain, along with Sarah's wild scream. It was her! Kelsey. Here! Finally home.

The same old Kelsey, but different somehow.

As Sarah rushed forward to hug her, Ethan took time to readjust his decade-old picture of the cute and curvy girl with wild bleached brown hair and whimsical green eyes. The adult Kelsey was trimmer with a neat brown cap of hair highlighted red. No longer cute but, rather, beautiful—stunning! The only disappointment lay in her eyes. While still as rich and deep as tropical seas, the whimsy was gone, replaced by the tired wisdom of one who'd seen too much, who carried a number of regrets.

Ethan could especially relate on this last count, and all because of Kelsey herself. The biggest regret of his life was that he'd let her get away.

Few in town probably realized their history, or recalled when they'd kicked their tight friendship up a notch. It had been the summer before their sophomore year and their crowd had slowly been starting to date. In Ethan's opinion Kelsey had possessed a sparkling personality, had been the prettiest girl in class and, unlike most, had always been up for a fevered game of basketball or baseball with the guys. Being such good friends and next-door neighbors, it had seemed natural to ease into some private little dates for swims, hikes and picnics to experiment with their affections, find out what a real kiss felt like.

It was all Ethan thought he'd ever want.

Until autumn, when he became a standout on the Whittier High football field.

He and Brad were the only sophomores on the varsity team and a few clever plays soon ensured their photos were splashed on the front page of the school paper. With celebrity came perks, like acceptance into upperclassmen cliques. Senior girls started calling— girls with cell phones and cars and big ideas! Brad handled it with poise, accustomed to feeling important due to Lewis's status around town. But Ethan went wild over the sudden attention. He eagerly accepted all invitations to picnics and parties, reveling in his new-found fame.

There was never an invitation for Kelsey, but she didn't complain when he shot off without her. In fact, she appeared to make light of the whole thing, pointing out that they weren't even going steady. But deep in his heart he suspected she might care a little bit, as he sometimes caught her watching him forlornly from her stoop as he hopped into a car full of kids at sundown. She didn't crack so many jokes anymore, either, or barge into the Taggert kitchen to help his mom bake a cake or join his folks in a game of poker.

Just the same, he was too preoccupied to worry about it.

By season's end, the football-hero novelty started to wear off. The upperclassmen decided that underneath the jersey he was just a kid after all and wouldn't fit in at their upcoming graduation parties.

Kelsey was indeed still his pal, albeit at a greater, more formal distance. By the start of the Christmas season, Ethan was desperately missing the romance they'd shared and decided to win back her affections.

Busy with his own social life for so long, he hadn't even noticed he had competition from his best friend, Brad. In hindsight, he realized there had been a few outward signs, like Brad treating Kelsey to a Hostess cupcake at lunch or offering her a lift home from school in one of the Cutler cars. But at the time, Ethan's attention was pulled in too many directions to piece it all together. He didn't get the total picture until the week before Christmas, at Brad's annual holiday party. Gathered round the Cutlers' giant decorated tree in the great room, small fun gifts were exchanged.

Brad whisked out several boxes for Kelsey but most of them could have been filled with sawdust for all Ethan remembered. The only gift that mattered was the silver friendship band Brad gave her.

And nobody but Ethan appeared the least bit surprised.

As Kelsey gleefully slipped the ring on her finger, it was clear he'd already lost her.

Maybe if she'd made a bigger fuss at the start of his ego trip, he'd have snapped out of it. Or more likely, he should've just known better in the first place.

After that, the best Ethan could hope for was a friendship with the happy couple, digging up girls for double dates, making-out with one in the back seat of one of the Cutler fleet, while Brad and Kelsey cuddled in the front.

Then eventually a cruel twist of fate had taken even that much away from him.

Since she'd left town, Ethan had worked to rediscover their magic with someone else. But, it had never happened.

Now the old temptation was back. And Ethan was left holding—of all things—the baby, a sobbing Amy Joy, whom Sarah had awakened with her squeals. He'd seen no option but to pluck her from the buggy and attempt to calm her.

He cuddled the squirmy, howling infant for what seemed an eternity—perhaps sixty seconds—before the girlfriends broke free and Sarah scooted over to take Amy Joy. Cradling the infant, she turned back to Kelsey to give her a closer look. Kelsey stroked the baby's head, remarking on how cute the dress looked on her.

"What's wrong, peanut?" Sarah cooed as Amy Joy continued to fuss. "Did that big guy scare you?"

"It was your screaming that scared her in the first place," he said, inspecting some drool on his freshly pressed uniform shirt to try and settle his nerves. When he abruptly looked up, he caught Kelsey's gaze. His heart shifted at the indecision there. She must be unsure about him, too.

It made it easier to take charge.

"Welcome home, Kel." With that simple greeting, he tentatively held out his arms. Miraculously, she slipped into them. As she pecked his jaw, he had to fight off a shiver. Seemed rude not to kiss her back, so he pressed his mouth to her forehead, the safest convenient spot.

Not so safe after all. The brief contact was enough to pick up her familiar body scent mingled with a sweet cologne. Heat rippled clear through him.

She pulled back, appearing more relaxed as she addressed the driver unloading her two suitcases from the storage compartment underneath the bus. Sarah, meanwhile, had put the wailing baby back in the buggy and was paying off the musicians.

The girls met back at point Ethan, now transformed into a dazed uniformed statue.

"I am so sorry, Kel," Sarah gushed. "I had planned to go over to the café with you, but Amy Joy won't stop crying so I should take her home. Can you drop by later? Anyone can tell you where we live."

Kelsey smiled. "I know where you live. The old Hawkins house on Earle Street. I recognized the address all along."

"Oh! Sure." Sarah looked sheepish as she gripped the buggy's handle. "Come over as soon as you can."

Watching Sarah zip off, Kelsey shifted awkwardly, aware of Ethan lingering beside her. She hadn't expected to be one-on-one with her special ex-next-door neighbor this soon. "Well, guess I'll go look up Mom."

Ethan apparently took this as a signal to grasp her larger suitcase.

"What are you doing, Ethan?"

"Coming along."

"Oh. You don't have to."

"I want to." His warm inviting smile suggested he truly did.

The Cozy Home Café was a mere half block down Harvester near Sixth Street. The Closed sign hung in the glass door but Kelsey jiggled the knob anyway. "She knew I was coming!"

Of course she must have known. But she hadn't mentioned it to Ethan, or likely anyone else, for the news had only hit the streets yesterday. Like Sarah, Clare probably worried about the negative fallout. She had good reason to be a little jittery. To this day there were people who wouldn't eat in her café because of the accident. Some because they were related to the kids who'd died, and others who merely hoped to please grief-stricken Lewis in return for a favor from his bank or newspaper. Ethan didn't believe Lewis was still pressing anyone to avoid the Cozy Home after all these years, but he wasn't openly endorsing the place either. Ethan had once offered to intervene with him on Clare's behalf, and she'd become very indignant, claimed she had plenty of business. He'd let the issue lie after that.

"She'll be right back," he said quickly, sensing Kelsey's dismay. "Look, there's a note saying as much taped to the glass. In the meantime, let's try not to leave a panic-stricken first impression." He gently guided her out of the doorway into the sunshine.

"As if I'm guilty of something, you mean?"

"Well, yes."

"So those scowls I'm spotting aren't squints in the sunshine. People are still upset with me over the crash."

He hesitated. "Not everybody."

"How many? Give me a percentage."

"I can't, Kel. It's not like there are town-hall meetings on the subject. I'm only suggesting you hold your chin up and smile, like a bright successful woman out for a walk with a bright successful man."

"You mean you?"

He tapped the badge pinned to his shirt. "Sure, me."

"Where will we go?" she asked bleakly.

"To the sheriff's office."

"Great. They'll think you're arresting me!"

That did it for Ethan. He busted out laughing.

"So you think that's funny?" She swatted his arm.

"Uh-oh, striking an officer. Now I do have reason to arrest you." He gently took her elbow. "Come along quietly and take your medicine. Which at the station, amounts to a very poor cup of coffee."

The police station was part of the municipal complex that took up most of Seventh Street. Kelsey decided the historic limestone courthouse at the corner of Harvester, with later additions running the length of Seventh, looked much the same as it had a decade ago. It was best described as patchwork architecture, last brought up to date in the seventies. The newer station and county offices, made of aluminum, steel and red brick, were utilitarian one-level extensions, with a mutual basement housing file rooms and jail cells.

Kelsey had seen the inside of a jail cell only once. After the accident she'd been hospitalized a week while doctors had tended her injuries—cracked ribs, severe skin abrasion, a broken arm, sprained ankle and a very nasty bruise to the head.

Sheriff Roger Norton, no doubt prodded hard by Lewis Cutler, haunted the hospital like a ghoul, taking every opportunity to pop in and interrogate her. Kelsey desperately wanted to help, but she simply couldn't remember anything. It was a kindly nurse named Nancy Farr who finally advised Clare to hire her attorney husband, Jacob, after she overheard Norton and Lewis Cutler discussing manslaughter charges.

Clare didn't believe they were serious until Sheriff Norton had tossed Kelsey in jail within an hour of her release from hospital. Clare had just gotten her tucked in bed with a bowl of hot soup and her TV remote when the doorbell rang.

He could hold Kelsey for twenty-four hours on suspicion of murder. It was up to her to start talking, confess to what she'd done.

That was when Clare phoned Jacob Farr. He oversaw Kelsey's official statement, which described being picked up in Brad's Jetta, stopping by the Cutlers' for some home movies and attending the grand march with all their friends. The prom itself was completely lost to her, as were the two hours leading up to the accident. Try as she might, she couldn't recapture those memories. The doctors concluded that, due to her head injury, she likely never would.

Kelsey was jailed the full twenty-four. Ultimately, the sheriff had no choice but to release or charge her. Meanwhile, her tough Madison attorney had badgered him and the county prosecutor to examine the plain hard facts on paper, and ignore Lewis Cutler's thirst for vengeance. Even if Brad had been teaching Kelsey to drive a stick shift that spring, nobody had seen her behind the wheel of the Cutlers' Jetta that night. While Kelsey had earned some speeding tickets driving her mother's car, she'd never been cited for recklessness. Kelsey had been no wilder than her peers, no matter what the petty rumors had said. In the end, Jacob Farr had convinced them a judge would blast their case out of court.

Now, as Ethan escorted her into the lobby of the station, she averted her gaze from the scarred black steel door that led to the cells.

"Uncomfortable?" Ethan asked gently.

Kelsey realized she was shuddering from head to toe. "I'm fine," she lied.

"Ready for some rotten coffee? Or maybe some water?"

"No thanks."

Ethan grinned, removed the suitcase from her grip, and set both pieces out of the way near the water cooler. "Come and sit."

Kelsey was about to take a chair near the clerk manning the front desk when Ethan protested, "Not there!"

The plump middle-aged blonde hung up the phone and glared at him. "What's the matter? I suddenly got rabies?"

Ethan studied her keenly. "Who'd dare bite you? Just so happens we were about to do a little reminiscing in my office."

"You can spare a minute." She reached over her desk for a handshake. "I'm Monica Blair."

"This is Kelsey Graham," Ethan introduced. "Fresh off the bus."

Kelsey took Monica's hand, noting a trace of recognition, but detecting nothing mean or judgmental in the woman.

"What brings you to town, Monica?"

"As it happens, Loretta Evensen is my cousin. When she lost her husband to cancer a few years ago, she invited me to come stay awhile. I did and decided to make it permanent. I'm sure you're wondering, why'd she leave the bright exciting city of San Francisco? Aside from the smog and high rent, I was lonely. Believe it or not, there are actually more straight middle-aged guys around here to choose from."

"She says all that strictly for effect, Kel," Ethan mocked. "She got here, spotted Mr. Hinkie, confirmed he owns the hardware store free and clear, then went straight back to Frisco to pack up her possessions."

Monica grew haughty. "The locals never call it Frisco."

Kelsey followed Ethan into his glass-enclosed office with some relief. No jarring memories for her in here. Sheriff Norton had kept this space mostly to himself during his tenure. Judging by the huge jar of red and white jelly beans on the steel-gray desk, the number of chairs stashed in every corner and the cork board full of kids' crayon pictures of him performing various duties, it appeared Ethan was a friendlier lawman.

He now gestured to a nearby chair, a metal one with a molded red plastic seat and back. After her journey by both plane and bus, it didn't look particularly inviting. But Ethan was now riding the front edge of his desk facing the chair, looking remarkably pleased with the arrangement. Fearful that any resistance would put their renewed alliance at risk, she sat down.

Clasping her hands in her lap, Kelsey smiled, taking her first close look at him. He'd certainly matured in the best possible way, lean and rugged, strong and sexy, his narrow mustache and neatly clipped brown hair adding to his good looks.

There were times… Times when she thought about Ethan, their lengthy history, their intimate knowledge of one another. Being next-door neighbors from birth left very little room for pretense. For a short while during their fifteenth summer, she had even figured Ethan could be the guy for her.

How fortunate that they hadn't gotten too carried away. It would have made his ultimate brush-off degrading and unbearable. Not that the rejection hadn't been painful. Suddenly their whole friendship had been devalued, their bond of trust weakened. Kelsey had managed to move on and soon ended up with Brad. But she had never forgotten how important it was to her to save intimacy for a truly solid relationship. Even with marriage plans in the works—for the summer after their freshman studies at UW–Madison—she'd made it clear to Brad they wouldn't be consummating their love ahead of the vows.

"A penny for your thoughts, Kel."

At the sound of Ethan's smooth warm baritone, she straightened on the crummy chair and gave a faint grin. Would he think her memories worth a penny? Had he even thought of her over the years? She wasn't emotionally prepared to handle fresh rejection, so she raised an entirely different issue.

"I was thinking about your career choice. You originally intended to major in business administration, didn't you?"

"That was my major. Then I settled back here after college not sure which direction to take. I juggled different jobs for a few years to make the rent, did some bookkeeping, sold insurance policies at Dad's agency, and worked evenings as a deputy under Roger Norton. When Norton announced his retirement near reelection time last year, it occurred to me that I liked the law-enforcement job a lot more than the others. So I ran for sheriff and won."

"Are you happy?"

"I find the job very satisfying. I enjoy the contact with people and they seem to respond to me well."

A small silence followed, both of them looking around as if not sure what to say next.

"Jelly bean?" Ethan abruptly swung his jar of red and white ones under her nose.

Realizing she hadn't had more than an English muffin and yogurt all day, she took a handful and popped some into her mouth. "These taste like the gourmet ones your mother used to buy."

"They are."

"So, how are your parents doing? Mom wrote me when they moved to Phoenix a few years ago."

Ethan nodded. "They left mostly to escape the snowy Wisconsin winters. They love the desert climate, the rock-garden yards. I'm concerned about them, though. The highways there are always clogged and the drivers extremely aggressive. Nothing like this sleepy town."

"But your dad spent years on the road selling insurance, so he's probably comfortable with it."

"So he says. Along with the reminder that they're only in their fifties—like your mom." Folding his arms across his chest he shook his head. "I'm probably overreacting but can't seem to stop myself, and figure it's just our turn to do the worrying. Some sort of karmic revenge."

And worry Kelsey did about her mother. "Is Clare doing all right, Ethan? I mean, really all right?"

"What exactly are you asking me, Kel?"

"Are people kind to her?"

He hesitated slightly. "Like all of us, she has her allies."

"Gee. I don't remember it ever coming down to allies."

"Nothing new, really. Kids just don't see it."

Of course. Adult life was all about friends and enemies.

"As far as I know, she's getting along," he assured kindly. " I'm in there almost every day—"

"Really!" she rejoiced.

He looked startled then pleased. "My favorite place for morning break."

Kelsey stared out the window, as if seeing a new ray of light on the horizon. "She claims to have her regulars, like she used to before the accident. But I've always been a little doubtful."

"She appears content, that's all I can be sure of." He looked at the floor now, as if self-conscious. "So, are you okay? Are you happy in Philly?"

Suspecting she'd be questioned over and over by classmates at the reunion, she'd prepared a cheery stock response about her life. But sitting alone with this once-cherished friend was enough to bring the plain truth of her situation bubbling to the surface. The loneliness, the disappointments, the depressing realization that her college friends had gone on to fulfill their own dreams of marriage and children. While she…

But these were hardly confidences to share with the first guy to dump her! Her pride wouldn't allow her to show dejection then, and still wouldn't.

"What's the matter?" he prodded. "The term *Philly* as offensive to you as *Frisco* is to Monica?"

"Nope. Philly's fine all around." She crossed her legs, mentally retrieving her original spiel. "My life is pretty hectic. I teach at a rather posh elementary school in the city and own a condo within walking distance. It's a tiny place that would cost a fraction here in Maple, but the location is so convenient, I don't even need a car. Great restaurants, parks and theaters are all within easy reach."

"Sounds this side of perfect."

She shrugged and smiled.

A surprising pinch of distress furrowed between his dark brows. But surely he'd wished her safe and well all this while. Hadn't he?

She would never know for sure what was on his mind as he broke eye contact and reached over his desk to push a button on an old intercom. "Monica, call the café, see if Clare is there."

As he released the button, Kelsey took him to task. "We could've called her ourselves."

"Naw. Monica loves playing secretary. That was her career back in Frisco."

The pair watched through the glass as the officious woman made the call. Hanging up the receiver she gave them a thumbs-up.

Kelsey rose to her feet. "Guess I'll be getting back. Thanks for the beans and the chat." When he levered himself off the edge of the desk, she added, "I've taken up enough of your time, but I'd like to keep my suitcases here for now though, if that's all right."

"No problem. In fact I'll be making my rounds soon, so I can drop off them off at the house."

"Great." With a nod to Monica, she was out the door.

Chapter Four

Ethan rounded his desk to take a seat, aware that Monica was already in his doorway, wearing a bright smile and brimming with curiosity.

"So she's the one, eh?"

With a rueful look, he pulled out his chair. "Why, oh, why did I ever confide my life story to you?"

"Because I'm one of the few ears in town who can give you impartial feedback. I'm also a good listener with a heart big as all outdoors. And your own ma is miles away."

"Yeah, guess that's why."

"It must have been a shocker to confront her so abruptly. Did you have any warning she was coming in on today's bus?"

"No," he complained. "Sarah could have told me but she didn't."

"Sarah's bound to be in a whirl, taking care of the baby, running the reunion. She probably doesn't realize how much it would matter to you."

"I'm not sure yet how much it does matter." He turned his chair to stare pensively out the window. "Guess I've thought about Kelsey most after each time a relationship's failed. Wondered if she could still possibly live up to my boyhood memories, if we'd be good together as adults."

"She seems very pleasant and likable, pleased to be here."

"I hope that sentiment lasts. She already caught some disapproving glares outside her mother's café. Obviously they hurt, but that's not to say she didn't handle things like a champ. She always was strong."

"You must be feeling pretty lucky all of sudden, having a second chance with the girl-next-door."

"It's far more complicated than it looks." Ethan tipped back in his springy chair with a groan. "Having her within reach doesn't change the fact that I totally bungled our whole relationship."

"Yeah, when you were a clueless boy." Monica earnestly leaned over his desk. "All teenagers fumble around when they're first learning the ropes. They love each other, burn each other, rack up the regrets. It's a learning process. Why, she doesn't even know how fast you recovered your good sense, that you already wanted her back when she was starting up with Brad."

"That's another problem. She managed to find the perfect replacement for me in Brad. She traded up bigtime, Monica. Brad was everything any girl could ever ask for, handsome, rich, smart. Even now, I can't live up to that image—or provide that sort of lavish lifestyle."

"Who says you have to? Kelsey's bound to have had all sorts of boyfriends over the past decade. None of them must have satisfied if she's still single."

"Maybe she's holding out for another Brad."

"Or maybe like you, she's merely searching for a sensitive person who makes her smile, and who she can rely on. It's up to you to show her that now you fit the bill. For the life of me I still can't understand why you never looked her up before."

Ethan grew silent as he always did when Monica tossed out that particular challenge. There was a good reason why he'd never chased after Kelsey, one he hadn't shared with anyone. Even now it pained him to think about it.

She simply had to come back on her own. And miracle of miracles, she finally had.

Just the same he realized if he wanted another chance with her, he would have to step up and face the same old risks and fears.

"Do you have any idea how long she'll be here?" Monica asked.

"No. Sarah wants to get her back for good, though, and will be working on her." The very idea warmed and excited him.

"Maybe that's what Kelsey wants, too, if she can make herself at home again without too much hassle."

"Whatever she wants, I've already decided I'm going to help her get it."

Monica's eyes widened. "Even if it puts you at odds with Lewis?"

"Yes, even then. I feel I owe it to her after everything that happened."

"Speaking of Lewis, he's called a few more times since this morning asking about Kelsey."

"Of course he has."

"What will you tell him?"

"Exactly what I know. That she seems healthy and happy."

"Throw in *kind* and *pretty*, too."

"Will do." Tipping his chair forward Ethan reached for the phone.

IN SPITE OF HER RATHER uncomfortable chunky heeled sandals, Kelsey almost skipped back to the Cozy Home Café. The Welcome Home side of the sign hung against the glass now. Anxious to see what changes had been made to the old place, she burst inside.

Stepping across the threshold was like diving back in time. Kelsey recognized everything, the booths upholstered in orange vinyl, the tables and countertops of white glittery Formica, the tan flooring, and the ceiling fans whirling lazily overhead.

A long lunch counter lined with stools and punctuated by an ancient cash register dominated the rear and that was where Clare Graham stood, flipping through a pad of guest checks, tallying figures with a pencil. As always, she was dressed in the same old aqua uniform shift accented with white collar and apron.

"Mom!" Kelsey cried.

Taken off guard, Clare turned sharply on the heel of her cushioned white shoe. "Hey, honey!"

It had been eighteen months since they'd seen each other, so Kelsey anxiously assessed her. The decades-old hairstyle never changed, of course, still a dark, shoulder-length curtain topped with feathered layers above the ears. But there were new startling differences. A mass of coarse gray strands now salted the black. Severe lines etched her eyes and mouth. At least ten pounds had dropped from a trim frame that couldn't afford it.

Clare Graham was a faded version of her former self.

Kelsey rushed across the scuffed linoleum to meet her halfway, cradling her tentatively, as if she might break.

Clare had no such fears as she squeezed her daughter close, cupped her face, soundly kissed her cheeks.

Eventually breaking free, Kelsey locked in on her mother's emerald eyes, swiftly welling like her own.

"Come and sit down," Clare invited. "We'll have lemonade and a nice long chat." As Clare went back behind the counter, Kelsey took a stool, knowing the cold drink would taste super. After all, little else had changed.

"So where were you, Mom? Just now."

"I was at the dentist for a filling." She shook her head as she carried full glasses over. "How I hate to close up like that midday. We're between the maple-syrup tapping and strawberry-picking festivals, but the odd tourist is still on the prowl. Can't afford to miss a one."

Clare had long assured Kelsey that business was good enough. Was that in fact true?

"So, you're good, honey?" Clare asked anxiously. Reaching over the counter, she took Kelsey's hand and put it to her cheek. Closing her eyes, she smiled. "This is great. Me and my baby girl."

A tightness pulled in Kelsey's chest. Acute homesickness had finally brought her back. Ironically, being here was making the ache all the worse. If only things could be like they used to be. If only…

They chatted until the creak of the front door and a burst of laughter interfered. Tourists. About fifteen of them, likely off the mid-sized motor coach now parked across the avenue.

Clare shifted into professional mode, dumping their lemonade glasses in the sink. Kelsey craned her neck to look into the silent kitchen.

"Don't you have *any* help here today? This is crazy!"

"I told Artie that I wouldn't be back this soon. He'll be in later."

"Artie Quail? Our old mailman is your cook?"

She nodded. "He got bored with retirement. As for Linda, she can be counted on ninety-nine percent of the time, but happened to call in sick today."

"What about Uncle Teddy? Can't he fill in?"

"He's not cut out for business, Kel. He's an artist."

Kelsey rolled her eyes but knew better than to argue. Clare's baby brother was a charming bachelor who'd taken over their mother's house after she'd moved out, and was still content in his forties to make a modest living playing piano in bars and lounges around the county.

"It's okay, Kel," Clare assured her.

"Sure it is," she returned brightly. "We can manage."

Clare gawked. "But you wouldn't know what to do anymore."

"Mom." Kelsey leaned over the counter to pluck a laminated menu from the back of a napkin holder. One glance confirmed that the food was unchanged, only a smidgen higher in price. "I remember exactly what to do."

Clare beamed. "There's a spare uniform in the back."

The hours melted as mother and daughter served a mix of tourists and locals. The latter group ranged from the curious to the openly disapproving. Kelsey fought to keep up a cheery front, treating everyone with the same respect, all the while wondering if she could ever hope for a measure of that respect in return.

It was 8:00 p.m. before Kelsey had finished cleaning the café kitchen and left Clare to ride out her last hour of business serving only beverages and desserts.

At ten past eight Kelsey was standing on the dimly lit porch of what used to be known as old lady Hawkins's house. Was it known around town as the young Yates house now? She doubted it. One name per home seemed the norm.

Sarah swung open the door promptly, as if she'd been on lookout. Scanning Kelsey's tight aqua uniform, she said, "Figured that's where you were."

"Sorry I'm so late, Sare," Kelsey said meekly. "Mom was in a bind."

Sarah held the screen door wide, rudely sniffing her guest. "I wanted a blast from the past and suppose I'm getting it."

"Sure, I stink of deep-fryer grease just like I used to. But I'm also bearing gifts from the fryer like I used to." She whisked a white take-out container from behind her back. "Onion rings *and* fries."

Sarah pushed the door open wider. "Come on in you stinker!"

Stepping through the front door into the living room, Kelsey noticed the Hawkins' faded striped wallpaper and fake Victorian pieces had been replaced. The walls were now a trendy moss shade, the furniture blue and cushy, the accent tables low and sturdy. There was also an entertainment center stocked with an outdated TV, stereo and speakers.

The baby cooing in the basket near the recliner obviously had precedence over electronics.

Kelsey rushed over, taking delight in the bundle that was Amy Joy. One look at the child's shiny eyes, drool-covered chin and flailing limbs had Kelsey spouting gibberish.

"Pick her up," Sarah invited.

She hesitated. "I think I'll wash my hands first."

"The bathroom—"

"I remember from when I fed the Hawkins cat during the old gal's vacations. Can't wait to see what you did with that antacid-pink bathroom."

"Uh, nothing. Yet."

"Oops, sorry." They both burst into giggles. Which prompted Amy Joy to join in with a sharp squeal.

"She's showing off for you," Sarah warned. "And wants out of that basket."

"There's one dream I can make come true," Kelsey vowed, moving down the hall.

Within minutes, the threesome was settled in the living room. Kelsey in the big recliner, her less-than-tidy uniform swathed in towels, cradling the baby. Sarah sat on the sofa, munching on the fried café food she'd heated up in the microwave.

"I saved some of this for Derek," Sarah said, between bites of onion ring.

"I hope so! The box was jam-packed."

"But I could eat it all myself," she confessed, licking her fingers. "My metabolism is like a furnace now that I'm nursing. But it would be torture for him to come home to this delicious smell and not get any." She made a face. "Marriage is full of compromises like that."

"So I hear."

"I shouldn't gripe about the little things. Actually, I'm very happy."

"As you should be." Kelsey gently tipped the baby against her shoulder and massaged her back. "From where I sit, you have it all, Sare, the job, the husband, the child. The things we intended to enjoy together."

"It isn't too late."

"But I've fallen way behind."

Sarah impulsively leaned forward in her chair. "If you were to move back, you could probably catch up in no time! Have you ever thought about it, Kel?"

"I guess I have, a little bit." Kelsey nuzzled Amy Joy's soft ear, dreaming of holding her almost anytime she pleased. "I wonder how hard it would be to settle back in?"

"It would take a little time to sort everyone out," Sarah admitted, "figure where they stand these days. Of course, there are the usual suspects you can already count on, Clare, Teddy, Derek. Not to mention Ethan. You had to be happy to find me standing on the street corner with him." She smirked. "We three were so close growing up."

"Did he really come to meet my bus?" she asked anxiously.

"Well, no, he just happened by. But I thought he seemed thrilled, didn't you?"

Kelsey wouldn't even hazard a guess. Ethan had abused her trust once too often.

"I'm certain he still cares for you, Kel," Sarah went on, perhaps sensing her uncertainty. "He always perks up when I mention your name and asks all sorts of questions about you. I've suggested more than once that he look you up in Philadelphia." She shook her head. "Somehow I just couldn't shake the hometown boy loose."

This didn't surprise Kelsey. After so much time spent incommunicado, he couldn't make the trip without encouragement, any more than she could muster the nerve to encourage him. "I would so badly like to trust Ethan again," she admitted. "But I worry about those old Cutler loyalties making things difficult."

"It does pay to be realistic about that, I'm afraid." Sarah slanted a nervous look through the screen door. "Ethan and Derek are both strongly attached to the old coot these days."

"I can't tell you how badly I'd like to hammer Lewis with some hard questions. How could he set Sheriff Norton on me? How could he thereafter boycott Mom's café if I didn't beat it out of town? How could he ever think I'd be careless with his son's—my own boyfriend's—life?"

Sarah bit her lip. "I have to warn you, Kel, Lewis may not be bullish enough to take an interrogation. He had a heart attack awhile back and apparently it makes him susceptible to more. You wouldn't want to be the cause of the fatal one."

"Surely there has to be a way to clear the air between us without my killing him."

"Considering the subject matter, it's going to be tough."

Suddenly the screen door creaked open.

"Derek!" Sarah greeted joyfully. "Finally!"

"Hey, babe. Kelsey."

Kelsey had watched the Yates couple's progress through a series of photographs e-mailed to her over the years, and she felt Derek had changed the least of anyone. He was still whipcord lean, had a full head of shaggy coal hair and an angular face, made all the sharper by his hard-knocks upbringing.

Looking weary in work-stained blue coveralls, he sauntered over to gently stroke his wife's head. "So did I miss any juicy talk?"

"Biggest thing we touched on so far is eccentric old Mrs. H.," Sarah claimed breezily. "Kelsey used to come here to feed her cat."

"So is Mrs. Hawkins..." Kelsey pointed a finger upward.

Sarah raised her eyes. "On the roof?"

"No, dummy. Dead."

"She's just over at the Healing Arms Nursing Home. Sometimes the poor dear escapes for an unsupervised walk and ends up back here, a bit disoriented. All in all, I think she's in good physical health and happy enough."

"That's good."

"So what's for eats?" Derek asked, eyeing Sarah's empty ketchup-smeared plate on the coffee table.

"Kelsey brought over some sinfully delicious rings and fries from the café."

"Oh," he said flatly. "You have anything else?"

Sarah flushed self-consciously. "There's meatloaf and salad."

Kelsey's heart fell as Derek strode off with a curt nod. Growing up, he'd been one of her best male buddies. She'd been, perhaps, one of his only true friends of either sex. Soon after his mother, Linda, had quit her domestic position at the Cutlers', she and Derek had started working at the Cozy Home Café. It had worked well for everyone, as the Yateses were hard workers and Clare had needed reliable help. But it had been common knowledge at the time no one else would hire Linda, due to Lewis's less-than-subtle inference round town that she wasn't satisfactory.

Derek had told her the whole sad story while they'd done dishes one night in the café kitchen. Linda had accidentally broken a 250-buck vase while she dusted. That had been it for her. She'd been out the door with no reference. A tough spot for a woman from the wrong side of the tracks, married to a lazy, violent drunk.

It had been Clare's faith in her that had made all the difference in the Yateses' lives. The café had become so much to the mother and son, an income, and a refuge from Chet Yates. Back then, Derek had been wild about the café food. He'd lived on it, quite literally. How bad could it taste now?

Sarah gave Kelsey's knee a consolatory pat. Pink with embarrassment, Kelsey changed the subject. "Tell me some new stories about your class. How is that little girl with the high IQ who tried to convince the kids her nanny was Mary Poppins?"

SARAH BID KELSEY GOOD-NIGHT at her front door around ten, inviting her to pop over to the gym tomorrow to help decorate it for the reunion festivities. Kelsey promised to think about it, but there was a real hesitancy about her. And Sarah knew exactly who'd put it there!

She went to the bedroom and put Amy Joy down in her crib for what she hoped would be a long nap but never was. She emerged in the hallway only to run smack into her husband, fresh out of the shower with one towel wrapped round his waist, another draped over his damp shoulder.

"That was a little awkward," she complained.

Derek toweled his glistening black hair. "Bound to be after so long."

"You do realize I mean you!"

"Huh?"

"That was no way to treat a friend! Refusing the café food you usually gobble right up. Avoiding eye contact. Leaving the room."

Derek gulped, suddenly looking half his age. "I didn't mean anything."

"You were a total grump! Care to explain?"

"Oh, I had a late call at the garage," he vented. "Some trucker stuck out on Route 12 broke a rod, which, of course, went right through the engine, meaning he needs a new one. I had to arrange a tow truck and give him a lift to the Empire Motel, all the while listening to his bitching. Then it was back to the garage to try and locate an engine, which I finally did. Not the way I hoped to end the day."

Sarah's steam evaporated then, like a kettle taken off the boil. "Just as long as you weren't acting out for Lewis."

"C'mon, Sare... Give me more credit, please." He gingerly dabbed his damp face.

"You can't blame me for being sensitive, when I have so much wrapped up in this reunion."

"You girls were bound to go overboard on it."

"It's as much for the guys as it is for the girls."

"No way."

"Really? Ethan seems interested. He's a guy."

"You know I hate to be compared to anyone else. I had a belly full of that as a kid, wearing clothes from the thrift shop, struggling to make the grade in class."

"You're getting too old to play the poor-kid-from-the-wrong-side-of-the-tracks card, Derek."

"You're the one dredging up the memories," he complained. "This house has been full of old school junk for months now. I'm sick of tripping over it day after day."

"Oh." Busy with so many things, this had blown by her. "Well, it'll be over soon. And none of it is Kelsey's fault. All she's done is show up."

His expression softened. "Sure, of course. You can relax, I'll do better next time. Now I gotta hit the sack, so I can get up early, fix that truck."

"Well, get Richard to help you. We're decorating the gym tomorrow and you're in charge of the lighting."

"I'll get there as soon as I can."

She folded her arms primly underneath her full breasts.

"Work-work-work, that's all you do."

"Remember, the quicker I pay off the loan from Lewis, the easier it'll be to feel independent." He tapped her nose and eased into the bedroom.

KELSEY ENJOYED HER FOUR-BLOCK stroll down the dark, quiet streets of the old neighborhood. After years in the bustling city, she'd forgotten how tranquil a warm summer night could be.

So Sarah wanted her home. That knowledge was as comforting as the velvet breeze hitting her face. It had been a small vague wish back in Philadelphia as she'd talked things over with Marta. But to actually be discussing the idea face-to-face with her best friend made it so much more real. Maybe it could work out.

The porch light was on at 223 Hilton Street, the white stucco, red-trimmed rambler where she'd grown up. Stepping through the front door onto the small square of tiles that served as a foyer, she immediately connected with her suitcases, delivered by Ethan as promised, jammed up against the small closet door on the left.

Fearing she'd trip over something in the dark, she stopped to get her bearings. Luckily, there were a couple of night-lights in strategic spots casting a helpful glow. With a resigned sigh, she confirmed that the living room furniture was unchanged. The tartan sofa sleeper and club chairs were still facing the stone fireplace, with stout wooden tables in between. The pieces were high quality, but as sorely outdated as the shiny olive-green drapes covering the picture window.

Clare and her stubborn battle against change!

Moving to the kitchen, she poured a glass of water and drank it, noticing the red-gingham motif, too, was just the same, right down to the rooster-print wallpaper.

Collecting her suitcases, she tiptoed down the hallway, passing Clare's room, already dark due to her early start. It wasn't unusual for her mother to get up at five to open the café by seven. As busy as she was, however, Clare had been thoughtful enough to leave a lamp lit in Kelsey's old bedroom at the end of the hall.

Crossing the threshold, Kelsey dropped her suitcases with a clatter and erupted in a shriek. There was a man in her bed!

A bespectacled man in hideous striped pajamas, propped up with pillows, calmly reading a book who, at the sight of her, tossed his book in the air and uttered an equally distressed wail.

"Uncle Teddy?" Kelsey moved closer. She hadn't seen him since they'd met in Cincinnati for a Graham family wedding. Blond, blue-eyed Teddy Rossbach had still been roguishly handsome then, playing piano during the church ceremony, and getting more attention on the dance floor at the reception than the young groom.

That had been six, perhaps seven years ago. This man was thicker in the face, neck and torso, his graying hair leveled in an unimaginative crew cut. Just the same, it had to be Teddy. There was no mistaking his melodious wail.

By now Clare had dashed in, cinching her yellow terry robe at the waist. "What's happened? What's wrong?"

Kelsey gaped and pointed. "What? What?" was all she could squeak out.

"Didn't I tell you?" Clare clucked in sympathy. "Teddy lives here now."

"In my room," cried Kelsey plaintively. She looked around for the first time to discover it was no longer her room at all but, done in masculine tones with some rather ugly modern furniture.

Clare grasped her shoulders from behind and nuzzled her neck. "It's not like I threw any of your stuff away. It's all in the basement. Bed, dresser, mementos, the works."

Kelsey couldn't get her mind around this shock. She whirled on her mother in bewilderment. "He had Nana's house to himself. A whole entire house."

Clare flashed Teddy an old familiar look of indulgence. "Too large for him, really, so we sold it and split the profits. Your nana approved, of course."

"I've been settled in here for months," Teddy explained, his big face cloudy with concern. "Sorry to upset you, pumpkin. We never expected you to show up again. Ever."

This stung a little, but Kelsey knew the teddy bear of a man wouldn't hurt her for the world. There was still no resisting his charm, either, his baritone so sincere and soothing, his bright blue eyes full of genuine affection. She wearily collected her suitcases. "Okay, Mom, where do I get to sleep?"

"I left linens out on the sofa bed for you. Didn't you notice?"

Clare escorted her to the living room like a fussy hen, unfolding the sleeper's creaky frame, plumping her pillows, inviting her to watch the old family television with the sound low. The prehistoric set had been built before remote controls were standard issue. It would have to do, as there'd certainly be no getting her Sweet Sixteen TV/VCR combo back, displayed so prominently at the foot of Teddy's bed, piled high with magazines, tapes and a bottle of Old Spice cologne.

"Teddy's been so good for me since Nana moved to South Carolina," Clare whispered as Kelsey set one of her suitcases on the coffee table and opened it. "He cheers me when I'm down. Plays cards with me on nights when he's not working the clubs. Massages the crick out of my neck with those big gentle hands. The companionship is nice."

And this from a woman who avoided change!

Kelsey paused, holding her nightie. "Do you ever go out anymore?"

"Of course. I go to the grocers, the druggist, the dentist."

"Mom, I mean do you ever socialize? Say, go to some of the piano bars while Teddy performs?"

"He likes to pick up women. How can he do that with his big sis along?"

"If you had a date of your own—"

"I don't date!" Clare hopped off the bed, tucking the covers with a sharper jab. "There simply isn't time for it."

"How much time can dinner and a movie take?"

"Too much."

"I always hoped you'd find a nice man."

Clare straightened up and looked around the room. "Where's your man? Where's my grandchildren? Yoo-hoo, come out, come out, wherever you are!"

Kelsey chuckled. "I surrender, Mom."

"Sleep tight, dear." Clare kissed her cheek. "Oh, and

thanks again for pitching in today. You're the ideal daughter when you quietly follow directions."

Accustomed to staying up till midnight even during the school year, Kelsey took her time washing up, then climbed onto the rickety bed and switched on the TV, adjusting the volume so it was just above the level of Teddy's snores.

Despite the disruption, he was already dead to the world.

Chapter Five

The journey had exhausted her, and Kelsey could think of no better excuse for sleeping in until after nine o'clock.

The first thought to hit her when she woke was that the café had already been open two hours. That kind of guilt was a longtime hazard of living under this roof. When were you going to the café? How long were you going to stay? Did you have a clean uniform?

Kelsey sat up on the creaky hide-a-bed in an absolute panic. She *did not* have a clean uniform! She wasn't sure if her mother expected her to help out today. Kelsey had to find out if she was needed.

Her old bedroom was only steps from the bathroom, so Kelsey couldn't resist peering in at Teddy. He was curled up, hugging a pillow. Judging by his smile, he was probably playing piano in Vegas, with his hero Wayne Newton.

Soon, Kelsey was scooting down the street in jeans and a knit shirt, clutching the uniform she'd worn yesterday, freshly snagged from the back clothesline. The ever-efficient Clare had apparently washed it at the crack of dawn along with a few others that Kelsey could never have gotten buttoned over her hips.

But how many daughters had a mother who wore size two? Kelsey at her leanest was a size six, but it felt just right. Healthy.

Flying through the café door about nine-thirty, she came to a quick halt in the center of the worn linoleum. The place wasn't exactly jumpin'.

"Gosh, Kelsey." An amused Clare rounded the lunch counter. "You look sixteen again—in a panic over being late."

"Well…" She trailed off sheepishly.

"You have no schedule to follow, honey."

"But I thought after yesterday—"

"Yesterday's gone," Clare stated evenly.

Kelsey paused, wondering if her mother was encompassing a lifetime of yesterdays, or simply the day before. It hurt a little as Clare took the uniform from her, apron and all.

"I'll just hang this spare back where it belongs," Clare said pleasantly. "Until the next emergency."

But, with Clare's small crew, who'd be around to pitch in next time?

Clare proved that she could still easily read her daughter. "Emergencies round here are a true fluke, honestly. Linda rarely misses a whole day." She looked uncomfortable now holding on to the confiscated uniform. "Of course I appreciate your help, but the last thing I want is for you to spend your visit working. We're managing fine."

Linda Yates was in the kitchen doorway now in regulation aqua, watching them, taking in their exchange. There was no mistaking her resemblance to son Derek with shagged jet hair, intense, observant dark eyes.

Suddenly erupting in pleasure, Linda scooted up and

demanded a hug. Kelsey obliged, enveloped in the familiar aromas of Linda's daily breakfast, fried eggs and cigarettes.

"How are you, Linda?"

"Can't complain."

"I should hope not. I've seen Amy Joy. You must be thrilled to be a grandma."

"You can bet your boots I am, and I love seeing Derek's happiness grow and grow, too. But I can't take any credit for that. It's all Sarah and the way she handles him." Linda glanced at the uniform in Clare's hand, then back at Kesley with some sympathy. "We're doing a big order for subs in back. Maybe you could run the front while we finish it. As long as you're here and all."

"No," Clare said firmly. "She's on vacation."

"But if I can be of help—"

Just then the front door opened and Ethan strode in. Although in uniform, he wasn't wearing his sidearm or a tie, but was sporting a beaming smile. Kelsey felt it lingered longest on her.

Linda raised a finger and jabbed at him accusingly. "See, Clare. See."

Hands on hard narrow hips, Ethan frowned at them. "What's up?"

"Nothing," Clare relented with a sigh. "Sorry, the subs aren't ready. Linda and I are about to finish them up. In the meantime, Kelsey will give you some coffee on the house, and anything else you may desire."

Ethan watched Kelsey approach the counter, her hips swaying gently, and knew what he desired most— some time with the girl in those tight low-cut jeans and a purple V-neck shirt. In hot and happy pursuit, he slid onto an orange cushioned stool. She was about to unwittingly fulfill an old fantasy by serving him his first cup of coffee of the morning. True, it wasn't across their own kitchen table and she wasn't worn-out after an erotic wrestling match, but it was something.

Kelsey brought two mugs and a full steaming carafe to the counter and poured expertly. Then asked him why he was grinning.

He took an appreciative sip, wondering where he could possibly begin. "I love your mom's coffee. And I was thinking how interesting your hair is now with those streaks of red."

"They're called *highlights*, Ethan."

"Very nice." His grin subsided a bit. "Rumor has it you pitched in here yesterday."

"The grapevine is still going strong."

His steady gray eyes locked on to hers. "How did it go?"

"There were several insulting penny tips, and a napkin bearing the blunt message Go Away."

"Who did that!" he demanded sharply.

"Relax, I'm not even sure."

Despite her bravado, Ethan could plainly see she was hurt. "Keep track of any more messages you get. I'll take care of them for you."

"It'll be all right. I plan to keep a sense of humor about it." She leaned down the counter and opened a glass-domed tray piled with pastries, her face lighting up. "Care for one? After all, what's a copper without a doughnut?"

"Hey, that's just a cliché."

"Your loss. Teachers love 'em with pride." She grabbed a bismarck for herself. Before she could replace the dome, he snagged the largest bear claw.

He grinned under her knowing look. "Always obey the teacher, I say."

"Since when?" Mustering a laugh, she sashayed off to wait on the few scattered customers.

There was an odd mix of patrons in that morning, thought Ethan. Beyond the few regulars there was a group of Clare's peers who never usually breakfasted on Harvester Avenue and some grumpy old men who always had their first coffee down at the barbershop. Listening to them talk confirmed his suspicions that they were here to get a look at Kelsey and pelt her with personal questions. Ethan was embarrassed by their nerve. It made him all the more determined to make things up to her, protect her.

She returned to the counter to ring up two guest checks at the register. "Look," she said to Ethan, "I get to keep the change." She opened her palm to reveal some coins.

He worked to match her smile. "How will you spend it? A trip to Tahiti?"

She lowered her voice. "Actually, I'm converting it to dollar bills as I go and stuffing it in Mom's emergency stash, which amounts to a terry-cloth slipper in her sock drawer."

"Statistics show that sock drawers are a poor place to hide your cash. Robbers often look there first."

Her green eyes twinkled. "Mom's not open to any new advice, I'm told, so I think it's best we leave the sock thing alone."

He sipped his coffee with pleasure. Ah, already, something they could do together.

Ethan was finishing a second cup of brew when Clare hustled out with the subs, neatly arranged in a bakery box. "You should keep these in the school fridge until you're ready to serve them," she instructed, shoving the box into his arms.

"Do I owe you anything?"

"Already paid for by the reunion committee, remember?" When he didn't budge, Clare asked him if he needed anything more.

"I wonder if you could spare Kelsey for a while—to help us over at the gym."

"Sarah mentioned the decorating last night," Kelsey admitted uncertainly. "But I thought I might be needed here again."

"Go along," Clare encouraged. "Enjoy your friends, do your share."

Ethan ushered Kelsey to the door. He'd originally intended to deliver the sandwiches to the gym and go on to the station to round off his uniform with holster, gun and tie. But now helping out at the reunion seemed much more attractive.

"Oh, Clare," Linda said suddenly, "I meant to tell you, the faucet in the restroom is dripping again."

As a surprised and fretful Clare marched off to check, Linda swiftly followed Kelsey to the door with a mumbled message. "We should talk, kiddo."

Kelsey stared at her. "Okay. I'll catch up to you soon, Ethan."

"Not now!" Linda snapped. "Tonight. Eight-thirty. Library steps." She whirled, just in time to confront a huffy Clare.

"The tap isn't dripping!"

"Well, count that among your blessings," Linda chided. With a regal lift of her chin, she headed for the kitchen.

Unlike most public buildings in town, the school

was located away from Harvester Avenue, in the heart of the oldest neighborhood, where a huge parcel of land had been designated early on for educational purposes. So it was reasonable for Kelsey to cross the sidewalk to the squad car at the curb.

Ethan expressed surprise. "You seriously want a ride on a beautiful day like today?"

"You have the subs, so I thought it would be more convenient."

"Let's take a walk, have a nice talk, just like we used to. Doesn't that sound fun? It isn't as if this thing is even heavy," he added, playfully lifting the box over his head in an Atlas pose.

"You drop those, buddy, and you'll be facing Mom all on your own!"

"They'll be fine. C'mon, we better get over to the school."

"Sure, Ethan, just like we used to."

Tucking the box of sandwiches under his arm like a bundle, Ethan matched her pace along the old cracked sidewalks, noting the way points of sunlight bounced off the dewy grass, bicycle bars, car fenders and Kelsey's reddish highlights. Towering several inches over her, he had a spectacular view of the sun dance in her hair.

"I'm surprised you're not married, Ethan," Kelsey remarked.

"Where did that come from!"

"Hey, you wanted to talk." She smiled sweetly up at him.

He acted slightly put out, but was secretly pleased at her curiosity.

"The question occurred to me yesterday on the street

as you cuddled Amy Joy," she went on to explain. "You always did have a way with kids, playing with them in the park, tolerating them at the movies. I always figured you'd jump at the first chance for a family."

"I do want to marry," he assured her. "But I'm not desperate enough to settle for just anybody."

"What happened with Carol Parker? Sarah mentioned in an e-mail that you were dating her."

"I'm not dating her now. Hardly ever did, in fact."

"Oh. Well, it did seem a funny match to me. She seemed a bit young for you and immature."

She was actually giving his love life some *very* serious thought—even more promising!

"It was a total mistake on my part," he quickly assured her. "Carol had just dropped out of college and came back here to regroup. She looked good to me, a fresh face in a town of not-so-fresh ones. Eventually, the novelty wore off and I realized we had nothing going on."

"I get the impression she's still nipping at your heels."

He grew uneasy now. "Not nipping, not exactly."

"But she's still interested."

"Maybe. That's the trouble with small-town dating pools, you know. It pays to think twice before starting something, as the person will be in your face forevermore! No matter what happens, no matter how badly it works out." He clamped his mouth shut then. Would she think he was referring to their little romance? He wasn't of course. She was the one mistake he long wished was still in his face—so he could make things right. Had her smile clouded over a little bit? It was difficult to tell.

"The rumor on the street is Mrs. Parker already picked out a mother-of-the-bride gown from the JCPenney catalog. Ordered it because it was on clearance and likely to disappear."

"No way!"

"Sarah never seems to get it wrong. Believe me, we agreed Mrs. P. really shouldn't have taken such a liberty."

"She sure shouldn't have!"

"If only because no firm date is set and the color brown could well clash with your bridesmaid dresses."

He was aghast. "I don't have any bridesmaids!"

Kelsey companionably clutched his free-swinging arm, resting her cheek against his solid bicep. "It'll all simmer down soon enough."

"Kel, do you really think I have a problem here?"

She chuckled. "No. I just couldn't resist winding you up. I hadn't realized how much I miss doing it."

Ethan calmed down, realizing her teasing had been an effort to recreate the old spirit between them. So was her interest in his love life sincere at all? He certainly hoped so. But it would pay to be patient, give her room to breathe. "I miss the jokes, too, Kel," he said. "But I miss the serious talks just as much."

"If it's any comfort," she consoled, "I'm no better at finding the right person myself."

Ethan's pulse leaped at the news. "Even with a much bigger pond to fish in?"

"Not even then," she confirmed self-consciously.

"So you really aren't dating anybody right now either?" he persisted. "Nobody important?"

She hesitated, then spoke in a nervous rush. "I was dating a younger person myself for a while, but for reasons you'd probably find strange."

"Try me."

"I had a pretty tense time in college, you see, due to

the accident, and I always wondered what I missed out on. So I thought I'd try and relive that time through my boyfriend, Tanner."

Ethan frowned. This was recent? Could she possibly still feel miserable about the crash? It tore him up to think so. "The accident wasn't your fault, Kelsey," he said quietly.

"*You* don't think so?" she asked bleakly.

He'd never given her any reason to believe otherwise. At least he'd tried not to. "This is no time to go into it, but it really wasn't."

She waved a hand in dismissal. "Anyway, the Tanner thing fell apart in no time. Instead of losing myself in his carefree life, I became bored and attempted to pull him into my more responsible one."

"Sounds like your instincts were guiding you back to reason."

"That's what I decided, too. Whatever I missed is lost forever. The only choice is to keep moving forward."

"Part of that progress was to come back here, then?"

She nodded. "I couldn't help that I didn't die in the crash along with Brad and the others. All I could do was live on, mature into a valuable human being. I'm finally coming to terms with my success, that I can make a valuable contribution through teaching."

It occurred to him that in her own self-destructive way, she had long carried the same burden of grief as Lewis. But unlike him, she was beginning to see light on the other side. If only Lewis could somehow do the same, accept that the living were left behind to somehow make the best of it.

Kelsey tensed slightly as they reached the school

grounds on Fairfax Avenue. She followed Ethan's lead along the property's concrete pathway, half listening as he pointed out improvements to the ball fields, ice rink and gymnasium.

She was bracing herself for what awaited inside. The last time she'd seen these classmates, they'd been mourning Brad and the other crash victims.

The domed cavernous building proved to be buzzing. People were grouping tables and chairs. Others were tacking crepe paper along walls and windows. Still others were assembling a gallery of memorabilia near the stage.

"It appears the girls outnumber the guys here about ten to one," Kelsey noted.

"Yeah, and that counts the two janitors scrubbing the bleachers."

By Ethan's pained expression, she wondered if he'd ever intended to stay and help. Had he joined in at the last minute for her sake, to help ease her welcome with their old friends? The very idea that he might be so thoughtful was extremely nice.

"I know a few faces right off," she observed lightly. "Beth Randall and Kim Gregson."

The pair was busy assembling a display. Beth was polishing trophies and Kim was rifling through some boxes on the floor. Beth took one look at her, nudged Kim with a frown and went back to polishing. Kim reacted quite differently, abandoning her project to happily approach. "Hey, Kelsey! I didn't know you'd be here!"

Kelsey embraced the tall skinny girl with clipped sandy hair who'd gone on to play basketball for an Ivy League college. Presumably, she now lived someplace else, so would not be directly involved in Maple Junction politics. A good choice to break the ice with.

"I settled in Los Angeles," Kim explained animatedly. "I'm a personal trainer to the stars! Well, not many real stars. Minor celebrities, mostly. The ones that dance and skate and run races in reality shows. And some former child actors. They're full of Hollywood stories, let me tell you!" She halted in midstream. "Here I go, yammering away when I'm supposed to be working on our sports display. We've got a great shot of you cheering at a football game, Kel. Can you still do the splits?"

"Yes," Kelsey said, mindful of Ethan's smirk. "I keep in shape."

"Go ahead and show us," he invited. "I'll handle the cheers."

Kelsey huffed in mock disgust. "Please tell me you have something on that display to embarrass this funnyman."

"Not yet," Kim admitted. "But I'll work on it. There are boxes and boxes of photos to mow through." With a wave she was off.

Ethan sauntered deeper into the action, drawing Kelsey along. They stopped near two of their old high-school teachers, Abigail Forester and Danielle Slade, who were studying the seating plan. Both ladies politely inquired about Kelsey's teaching job in Philadelphia and she was quick to praise them as good role models. This drew them into an animated discussion on today's more permissive parents and the impact of technology. In the meantime, Ethan took a pen out of his blue uniform pocket and scribbled on the chart held by Danielle, moving his name and Kelsey's to a table with Sarah and Derek and crossing them off their original, less appealing positions. Old cotton-topped Abigail didn't approve of his trick but Danielle laughed it off, said it would be fine.

Eva Thompson, who had suffered the stigma of getting knocked up in their junior year also greeted Kelsey without rancor. Kelsey was always glad she'd given her ostracized friend a baby shower back then. Not only had it been her only shower in the whole scandalized town, but Eva had supported her in return a year later. The night before Kelsey had left on the Greyhound, it had been Eva and Sarah who'd taken her to the woods for a bonfire. They'd laughed and cried, roasted marshmallows.

The only thing missing had been Brad. And Ethan.

"Not so bad after all, is it?" Ethan murmured insightfully.

Ethan was having so many correct hunches about her it was as if he'd managed to plug back into her psyche. It was flattering, but also a little spooky after all their time apart.

Sarah was scooting toward them now, dressed in pink sweats and tennis shoes, her golden hair in a ponytail. The reunion boss lady was in a frazzle. Her gaze fell sharply to the box under his arm. "Where have you been? What have you done to those sandwiches!"

Ethan reluctantly retrieved the box. "I guess I crushed them under my arm on the walk over. But it's all you two girls' fault!"

"How?"

He lowered his voice. "Kelsey was giving me the scoop about a certain dress ordered from JCPenney."

Sarah groaned. "Kelsey, that was told to me in confidence."

Kelsey stared off with an unrepentant air. "I was only having a little fun with him."

"Well, find another way that doesn't involve the rest of us."

Kelsey couldn't help notice that Ethan seemed to enjoy that suggestion very much.

Ethan began to jangle as he handed Sarah the box. He dug his small flip phone from his pants pocket and announced that it was the station. Sarah nodded and flounced off with the subs.

"Yeah, Monica," he answered. "I do know where my radio is. In the squad. No, I'm not in spitting distance. Wally McClean's in the car answering your calls? Send Nate to stop him, and tell him to be kind. Wally's been on the slide since his ninety-second birthday. I am getting there." He winked at Kelsey. "So why were you calling me in the first place? Oh, that report is in my desk. Check the bottom drawer. I'll wait."

Deciding to leave him to his call, Kelsey pointed in the direction that Sarah had taken and went after her.

Kelsey found Sarah in the small room backstage that sometimes served as a kitchen. With just a domestic-size fridge and stove, it held only the bare necessities for storage, but there were plenty of stainless-steel surfaces for caterers' prepared food, which was the preferred arrangement for events hosted here. This was due to principal Ed Chamberlain's influence. During his long tenure he'd fought many a board and PTA to keep the gym's focus on athletics, rather than making it a hospitality hall for shameless fund-raising.

"A gym should smell like dirty socks," Kelsey bit out in a gravelly voice to the figure half-concealed behind the fridge door. "Not wussy chicken à la king. And what will happen when somebody's wedding reception clashes with an important basketball game? Will the lure of money win out over school spirit?"

"Very good, Kel," Sarah responded with a grin, popping up to shut the fridge with her hip. "You know, for a minute, I thought he was really here."

"Yeah right. What did they always say about Chamberlain? Often imitated, but never too well."

Despite her ribbing of the principal, Kelsey, like many others around town, agreed with his policies. But as usual all that ever mattered was that Lewis Cutler backed him. In return for a bronze-and-wood plaque displayed in the gym honoring Brad's athletic abilities, Lewis made a special yearly donation to help pay the utilities and upkeep.

Now that same plaque rested unceremoniously on the steel table in the kitchen, beside the box of squashed sandwiches.

As Kelsey traced a finger over Brad's name on the engraved brass, Sarah came to stand beside her. "That's only in here temporarily, while we're decorating, so it won't get damaged."

Kelsey smiled faintly. "It seems totally against the law of nature for a young person like Brad to die. He was so full of potential, I sometimes wonder what he'd be like now, what contributions he would have made. If we'd be as happy together as we thought we would be."

"Dwelling too much on any lost love has got to be unhealthy."

"I've finally figured that out. I was just telling Ethan how I intend to move on for good. After I tie up some nagging loose ends."

"Assuming Lewis is the most nagging loose end—"

"He is."

"I was too pushy warning you off Lewis because of his health. If he still has the strength to protest your return, you should have the right to confront him."

Kelsey grew slightly defensive. "It could be a positive experience for him if he approached it with a good attitude."

Sarah didn't look too hopeful. "It might help to use a go-between to smooth the way. An ally to both camps, who could talk to Lewis first on your behalf."

"Like Ethan?" Kelsey guessed.

"Yes. What do you think?"

"It might work."

"But you're not sure."

"I would like to take a little more time to get to know Ethan again before I trust him with such an important task."

"I'm beginning to sense that Ethan hurt you more than I ever realized."

"Maybe my expectations were too high. I don't know."

"Derek also qualifies as a go-between, but he doesn't have Ethan's patience," Sarah continued, "or his way with words."

"I'll keep both in mind for the job. Speaking of Derek, he seemed out of sorts last night. Is he angry at me?"

"Gee, no. He had a hassle at work is all. He comes home tense like that lots of nights. You'll see, he's still wonderful all cleaned up and relaxed."

"Good. I'd hate to lose his friendship."

Sarah squeezed her tight. "Don't you worry, just hold on to the dream."

Kelsey and Sarah rejoined the workforce on the gym floor to find Ethan standing centerstage, staring upward, talking to someone concealed behind the curtain. The girls skipped up the stage stairs to discover Derek was inspecting the lighting system. He looked far more relaxed and ten years younger today in jeans and gray T-shirt. He smiled directly at Kelsey now and it made her heart melt. This was the sweet, edgy guy who'd worked the café with her and had proclaimed himself the brother she never had.

"I think what we need around here is the kid who normally handles the lights," Derek grumbled with a grin.

"But that used to be you," Kelsey protested. "Every play, every assembly, every choir and band concert. You can't tell us this high school has gotten any new switches or anything."

Derek smirked. "Nope. It's just as Ben Franklin installed it."

"Every circuit seems to work," Ethan said, gazing up, then over at the girls.

"Seems to?" Derek challenged.

"It isn't thoroughly tested yet," Ethan claimed. Taking a hand off his hip, he extended it to Kelsey. "Hey, partner, c'mere."

Kelsey put a hand on her heart with a squeak. "What are you up to?"

He made a small lunge. "You were my female lead in Whittier High's best performances of the nineties, weren't you? The beauty to my beast?"

"I can't remember the last time I danced."

"Neither can I."

Feeling a little shy, she moved into his open arms. Humming the theme song to *Beauty and the Beast,* he began to twirl her round and round with ease. She allowed him to glide her across the floor, sweep her away to simpler times when they were dancing onstage in full costume.

Derek joined in the fun by bathing them in colorful splashes of light while some of the reunion crew gathered round to watch and sing the lyrics.

Eventually, Kelsey allowed her eyes to drift shut as she put her complete trust in his lead. Letting her tensions melt away, she relived the show's dramatic conclusion when he slipped off the brown suede mask he wore as the Beast, and transformed himself into the perfect prince.

That was the boy she'd loved so well, the man she now wanted to believe in.

The magic ended all too soon. The gym went quiet as Ethan posed her in a dip. She opened her eyes to find him gazing down at her with a powerful gleam in his. Her heart fluttered furiously.

"That was beautiful!" Sarah scampered closer, clasping her hands. "Hey, wouldn't it be fun to recreate that number to kick off the banquet program? We could round up some of the rest of the old cast to dance again in the background. Are any of them here today?" Kim Gregson's hand went up, as did Eva Thompson's. Both were willing to participate and promised to contact some of the others.

"We'd need a rehearsal, costumes," Kelsey protested.

Ethan had righted her onstage but still held her hand. "Let's try it. Please, Kelsey?"

She smiled. "Okay, if you want. If fact, we could practice right now."

Suddenly, Ethan's cell phone rang again. He glanced at the caller ID. "It's the station. I really have to go this time." He wistfully touched her cheek. "We'll get it done." With that, he dashed down the stage steps and opened his flip phone.

Kelsey watched him leave, taking the magic with him.

Chapter Six

Ethan had dinner with the Cutlers every week. It was usually a relaxing treat for everyone, savoring delicious food, catching up on town gossip and business. He even turned his cell phone off.

As he rang the mansion doorbell tonight, however, he had mixed emotions. He simply couldn't get his mind off Kelsey. What a day they'd had! Slipping easily into their old roles, walking over to the school, mingling with pals. He'd initiated that impromptu dance just to hold her. They'd moved so fluidly together, just like before.

Staring into her eyes as he'd held her in that final pose, his heart had almost leaped out of his chest. All his buried feelings for her had bubbled to the surface, all the raw hopes and dreams he'd harbored for her as an innocent kid.

Leaning over her, cradling her in midair, it had taken all his self-control not to crush his mouth against hers, finally kiss her with adult skill and appreciation.

He was certain she'd felt something too. Would she be willing to admit it? Would she be willing to give them a second chance?

He wondered how much time he had to win her over,

make it worth her while to choose Maple Junction over Philadelphia. The reunion was coming up fast and would be so brief. He would have to seize every opportunity to move closer, as he had today with the dance routine.

Now, he was about to end this perfect day by dining with Kelsey's biggest foe. While he didn't wish to hurt Lewis, he'd run out of patience with the old man's grudge against Kelsey. A grudge that should never have become a part of Lewis's grieving process.

Somehow, Ethan had to make all of this right for everyone. It wouldn't be the same without Brad, but it could be a whole lot better.

With some reluctance, he rang the doorbell a second time. It would be too much to hope nobody was home.

At least the coy and clingy Carol Parker wasn't on duty this evening. It was Bailey herself who answered the bell.

"Come on in," she welcomed with friendly impatience, pulling the heavy door open wide. Like his other friends' folks, they'd long ago encouraged him to enter without knocking. While it seemed natural at other more modest houses, he couldn't quite do it here at the imposing mansion where there was always a clear air of formality, an almost reverent silence and bustling staff.

Ethan was surprised to hear unfamiliar voices in the study off the foyer. As he moved to check it out, Lewis appeared in the doorway.

"Ethan!" Lewis jovially clapped his hands. "Didn't realize the time."

Ethan was close enough now to glance into Lewis's domain. He spotted two college-age guys moving around a worktable covered in papers. "Are you in the middle of something?" he asked.

"Sort of."

"I can come back another time."

"Nonsense." With unexpected joviality, he clapped Ethan on the back. "Come along. Let's eat."

The expansive dining-room table held its customary lace tablecloth and candelabra with three place settings of crystal, silver, and blue china near one end. Lewis sat at the head with Ethan on his left, Bailey to the right, nearest the swinging kitchen door.

"So what's this I hear about an addition to the reunion program?" Lewis's face still wore a pleasant smile but his voice was tighter.

Ethan was startled. He barely had his napkin in his lap and the housekeeper, Ruth, was serving him thick beef soup full of vegetables. He forced a grin. "It's true. Nothing fancy, just a dance."

"I intended to say a few words—"

"Oh, it won't interfere with the speeches," Ethan hastened to assure him. "It'll be at the top of the evening." He spooned some soup and tried to savor its potent meaty taste. But tonight's underlying tensions were working against his appetite.

"So Derek's wife has a whim and everyone follows," Lewis grumbled.

"Actually, it was my idea."

Lewis gripped his water glass, his eyes wide. "Yours!"

"Yes," Ethan returned mildly. "I was helping Derek test the lights and started to dance. Before long, everybody was crowding round—"

"Crowding round you and Kelsey Graham."

"Yes, Lewis. We were partners in many school productions."

"Try your soup, Lew," Bailey encouraged. Smiling at Ethan, she gestured for him to eat, too. "Reunions are supposed to be lively and joyful. Perhaps the dance will be fun."

"Brad and I never thought much of the drama club," Lewis blurted out.

Ethan glanced at him in surprise. "Excuse me?"

"Well, it's not preparation for the real world like team sports are. You have to admit, you learned more about competition and strategy playing football and hockey."

"You can't be serious! There are very valuable life lessons to be gained from acting, such as poise, self-confidence."

"Well, Brad already had those, didn't he?"

"This isn't about Brad, Lew. I'm only making the argument that there's room for sports and the arts in any high-school curriculum."

"It just seems to me there should be time for sports highlights at the banquet, if there's room for the cha-cha."

So this was about Brad after all.

"There is plenty of memorabilia on show honoring the sports teams," Ethan replied. "I saw some it of myself over at the gym. Brad is well represented."

"But nothing live-action. It's all pictures and trophies. The choice of priorities seems a shame to me."

Ethan shrugged. He was proud of his school participation in the arts. It had made him one of the better dancers at college parties, even earned him some prize money in dance contests. But more importantly, at the time it had given him exclusive access to costar Kelsey. He wouldn't trade those experiences for anything.

"Drink your wine, Ethan," Bailey urged, as she

might encourage a child with milk. "It's the Minnesota Riesling you like so well."

Bailey diverted the conversation with chatter about her work on the park committee as they plowed through their first course. "There is room for another garden along Heron, across from your apartment, Ethan. Daffodils would be nice. Such bright colors."

"Not many tourists wander along Heron," Lewis objected, "being on the backside of the park. They generally stick along Harvester and the side streets."

"It isn't my intention to impress outsiders. It's beauty for us, darling."

Lewis smiled then and reached across the lace to pat her pale bejeweled hand. "Nobody knows more about beauty than you, my love."

Ethan watched Bailey glow in the candlelight. Under his gruff businessman's exterior, Lewis was always capable of tenderness with the opposite sex. If only he could extend some to Kelsey again.

Ruth and her daughter Carmen came through to serve. Bailey requested more wine and extra rolls for Ethan.

The salad proved crisp and green as always, with a ranch dressing whipped light with fresh buttermilk, but Ethan struggled to enjoy it.

"How is your mother, Ethan?" Bailey asked. "I always miss her when I garden in the park. She loved it so."

Ethan told them a funny story about a lizard Mom had found in her kitchen cupboard. "She screamed so loud the neighbor almost called 911. But Dad quickly grabbed the thing by the tail and brought it out to show everybody."

"So many reptiles in the Southwest. I could never be happy there," Lewis mused chuckling.

Bailey laughed, too. "You could never be happy any-place but here."

The main course was juicy peppercorn-coated ribeye steak and scalloped potatoes.

It finally dawned on Ethan that they were eating all of his favorite dishes. Lewis must be trying to fatten him up to put him in an agreeable mood for some reason.

Predictably, dessert turned out to be cheesecake with raspberry glaze, Ruth's specialty. Carmen served slices no doubt cut by her mom, for each one was a custom size. Bailey's was a sliver, Lewis's slightly larger, and Ethan's a handsome wedge. Ethan winked at Carmen and she giggled, dashing back through the swing door.

"It isn't an election year," Lewis retorted to her disappearing back.

Ethan knew Lewis didn't believe in other people getting familiar with the help, but Ethan never let it stop him.

Ruth brought coffee. Then finally she returned with brandy, setting a snifter near Ethan, a snifter and ashtray by Lewis.

"Anything for you, Mrs. Cutler?" Ruth asked.

"No thank you, Ruth."

Then Lewis gave his wife a significant look.

"Excuse me," Bailey said, rising. "I have some things to do upstairs."

"Drop by the study and tell the fellas to knock off for tonight. I'll see them tomorrow first thing. I mean 6:00 a.m."

Bailey sighed. "Yes, Lewis, you would mean six." Leaning over Ethan, the graceful woman kissed his cheek, accepted his thanks and strode out.

Ethan could sense a man-to-man talk about Kelsey was coming. Full of his favorite foods, presumably he would be relaxed and ready to face Lewis. He watched as Lewis thoughtfully exchanged his dessert plate for the ashtray. Planting a cigar between his teeth, he ignited it with a crystal lighter. Puffing it to life, he leaned back in his chair. "So how has life treated Kelsey?"

Ethan met his eyes steadily. "She's turned out responsible and pleasant."

Lewis leaned sideways into the table with a disconcerting jerk. "So have you figured out her motives yet?"

Ethan was taken off guard. So it was the agenda issue again. "I just don't understand what you think she's up to, Lew."

Lewis scowled. "Well, I wouldn't know, would I?"

Despite the forceful tone, Ethan found his response pretty lame. It was so unlike Lewis to talk in circles and riddles this way. What could be causing the old man's distress? Was it merely a festering resentment for Kelsey? Or something more?

On the other hand, maybe it was only Ethan's clinical cop mind going into top gear. He had a tendency to overanalyze suspicious behavior.

"Even though I think the dance number is silly," Lewis went on, "I do appreciate that you've managed to move in on the girl so quickly."

"I didn't do it for you," Ethan asserted with some impatience.

Lewis reared slightly. "Oh."

"I like Kelsey. She's a friend. I miss her."

Lewis paused, his brows furrowed in thought. "I'd hate to think she could ever come between us."

"That will be your decision, not mine."

"I am trying to advise you to proceed with caution and you're not listening."

"I'm listening, I just don't understand."

"I'd like a better picture of what she's up to. How is she behaving? What is she saying?"

"It's all normal, nice conversation. She's back to visit family and friends. It's that simple."

"She's mentioned nothing about the accident?"

"She still feels bad about it."

"How's her memory?"

"I assume it's just the same."

"You assume?"

"We didn't discuss it. It stands to reason she still has a gap of several hours that she can't fill."

"So exactly when *is* she returning to Philly?"

"I don't know that for sure yet."

"Well, keep your defenses high and your ears open. If anything seems peculiar, report back."

"You wouldn't by any chance want to meet with her yourself?"

"I couldn't possibly bear the strain."

As Lewis clutched his chest, Ethan thought he had a lot of nerve trashing the theater. He was a master of drama when it suited him.

"You aren't leaving!" Lewis complained as Ethan rose from his chair, leaving his brandy untouched. "I thought we could play some chess. We usually do."

He managed a crooked grin. "I need to take my Beast costume to the cleaners before they close."

Lewis's voice rose in tinny disbelief. "You still have your old costumes?"

"My mother kept them, then stashed them in my

storage closet when she moved. Lucky break, eh?" On that cheery note, he walked out.

As he passed through the foyer, Ethan glanced at the study to find it dark. He wondered what the young guys were working on but didn't feel comfortable spying on Lewis. And if Lewis caught him in there with the light on, he'd end up playing chess after all and be trapped for another two hours.

Sitting in his squad car, he had the overwhelming urge to hear Kelsey's sweet sexy voice. Reconnect with her again before bed. He flipped open his cell and punched in Clare's number. No answer. So where was she? He felt a territorial jab. She had a right to be anyplace, all grown up, with no commitment to him. But still, he wondered.

THE MAPLE JUNCTION Public Library was located on the corner of Harvester Avenue and Second Street, directly across from the park.

Kelsey approached on foot that evening as the library clock chimed the half hour. Eight-thirty on the dot. Linda was waiting as promised, seated at the edge of the library's bank of stone steps, half-hidden in the shadows beyond the reach of the nearest streetlight. But she suddenly lit up in vivid silhouette against the flame that shot out of her old reliable Zippo.

As the cigarette dangling from her mouth ignited, the whole picture had a covert feel to it. *The Spy Who Wore Aqua.*

Kelsey settled down beside her on the cool stone.

Linda inhaled deeply, then appreciatively blew out a stream of smoke. "Ever take up smoking in the city?"

"Tried it. Hated it."

"Good," she rasped. "It's a vicious habit. Derek finally gave it up. Sarah made him, as soon as they got serious."

Kelsey wondered for the umpteenth time what this meeting was about. But Linda deserved a bit of her time and patience. "That marriage sure turned out well," she offered.

"Didn't dare to ever dream *that* big for the boy!" Linda crowed like a lottery winner. "He was always so sullen, with a giant chip on his shoulder." She grimaced now. "All those years he drank, Chet was so harsh to us, physically and verbally. Might sound mean, but I was relieved when a seizure took the buzzard." She glanced over at Kelsey through a smoky haze to gauge her reaction.

"Folks know you had it rough." Not that many had extended a helping hand. But Linda had faced every reality with a tough attitude Kelsey admired. And wished for in her own mother, Clare, who always fretted too much over what people thought.

"It was a whole new beginning for Derek and me after that. Free of Chet's abuse and neediness."

"The autumn of our senior year."

"Right. With Chet in the ground, Derek was able to catch up on his studies, scrape enough passes to graduate with your class. Then old man Cutler helped him take over Mel Trumbull's garage, find rooms of his own on the right side of the tracks, so people would trust him repairing their cars. One miracle after another."

"Some were surprised that you chose to stay over on Coach Road by yourself."

"Nothing I ever wanted more after a long day at the café than to go back to my bitty house. And like I always figured, the wrong side of the tracks could be a paradise Chet-free, so empty and peaceful. By the time Derek moved on, we had the place all cleaned and painted, had bought new furniture from the outlet store on the interstate during one of their no-interest-till-doomsday promotions. It was the best summer of my life, working alongside my boy to spruce things up. The summer of freedom." Linda stopped abruptly then and squeezed Kelsey's knee. "Sorry, hon. Here I'm running on about what must have been the worst summer of your young life."

Kelsey nodded.

"I have always cared, watched you close over Clare's shoulder. We're like sisters, her and me. Rising above prejudice, heartache, managing to keep our dignity. Raising our kids round the bustle of the café."

"I figure you have something you want to tell me, while Mom is trapped there closing up."

"Well, that la-di-da education ain't a bit wasted."

Kelsey was growing edgy now. "What's up, Linda?"

Linda stood, dropped her cigarette butt and crushed it under her utilitarian shoe. "Let's go for a walk in the park."

After a long day on her feet, Linda crossed Harvester with amazing agility. Kelsey was on her heels as she plunged between two bushes.

The grassy retreat was a square block large, supplied with a fountain, gazebo, playground equipment and benches. Mother Nature was well represented with floral gardens, shrubs and an inordinate number of sugar maples. As they followed a paved walkway dotted with pretty gas lamps, Kelsey nodded to strolling couples, ignored benches holding frisky ones and exclaimed at the improvements she noticed.

"All Cutler's doing, of course. Just like this is Cutler's doing," Linda said, grasping Kelsey by the shoulders and turning her forty-five degrees toward Second Street. "I assume you didn't know?"

Staring three hundred feet through the trees, Kelsey's heart nearly stopped. In the blackness tucked away at the deep end of Second Street flashed a big green neon sign: Doo-Wop Diner.

The Hansons' dumpy old deli was now an inviting sit-down restaurant.

She groaned as the implications sank in. Clare's modest establishment had flashy competition for liquor-free, homespun casual dining.

Cutler's doing as Linda had bluntly admitted.

Apparently, Clare had avoided the threat of a boycott by sending Kelsey away, but still got socked where it hurt.

"How long has it been there?" Kelsey demanded tersely.

"Ten years."

"You mean to say this place popped up right after the car crash?"

"The transformation took a few months, but it was open soon after you started college."

"Why didn't somebody tell me?"

Linda grimaced. "I voted to tell you right off the bat, so did Sarah. But Clare said no. She convinced us you'd only worry and she could handle the competition. Sarah and I went along because we believed her. And, like Clare, we figured you already felt guilty enough. Makes sense when you think about it, no way could you have returned, or fixed things."

"How does Lewis fit in exactly?"

"You can probably connect most of the dots yourself.

Lissa Hanson's dead in the car accident along with Brad and Todd. Todd's family quickly ups and moves away. Heartbroken Lewis moves in to grieve with who's left, Larry and JoAnne Hanson. He finds out about their dream to have a fifties-theme diner."

"I never heard that dream," Kelsey said flatly.

"Well, neither did I, but it could be true they had it. Anyway, they started by closing and gutting the place. Then Lewis brought in an architect from Milwaukee to sketch out a plan. Other outsiders followed to do the actual work, the decorating and construction. Suddenly, one day there was a whole new place to eat."

"Clever plan," Kelsey fumed, "strong-arming Lissa's parents into wanting a dream that would directly hit Mom, hiring impartial workers who weren't swayed by loyalty or emotion. As if driving me off wasn't enough."

"It could be the Hansons' dream was not only real, but just happened to threaten Clare's," Linda protested. "It could be Lewis only wanted to lighten their grief because he understood it so well himself."

"Maybe..." she begrudged. "How exactly do Lewis and Bailey treat Mom?"

"Civilly, with a this-town-is-big-enough-for-all-of-us attitude. But it's never been the same as it was before the crash. I'm still never sure what they're up to behind their superior smiles."

"Don't tell me they're still working against Mom somehow."

Linda jammed another cigarette into her mouth and lit it. Kelsey sensed this was a stall tactic and waited.

Sure enough, Linda took a few long puffs and spoke again. "That's a tough call to make. For instance, the Doo-Wop has expensive weekly ads in the *Cutler Ex-*

press. Seems unlikely an eatery in a small town would sink that kind of cash into promotion. It's overkill. People already know the restaurant and their menus. Also, the Doo-Wop always caters the big civic events. And the chamber of commerce gives them a nice mention in the tourist brochure."

"So behind the honeyed smiles, the Cutlers continue to undercut Mom's business," Kelsey sputtered.

"Hard to know exactly how much blame they deserve," Linda said uneasily. "With the extra complications."

Kelsey gaped. "Meaning?"

"The café does have weaknesses. Starting with its hours." Linda gestured toward Second Street. "See those cars at the curb. The diner's open seven till eleven every day. The Hansons don't even close on Sunday like Clare does."

"No way Mom can compete with that!"

"Of course she can't. But it's easy to see why and how the Doo-Wop does better. Their bigger crowds bring in bigger profits, so they can afford more help to cover the diner for longer hours. Plus, JoAnne Hanson ain't a widow like Clare. Larry is a good, strong male partner to lean on."

"Is Teddy really so hopeless?" Kelsey asked in desperation.

"Heavens, yes! He's tried, Kelsey, but food service isn't his thing. He gets entangled with the ladies, drops dishes and mixes up orders. It's best he stays away." Linda leaned against a large tree, looking tired. "On top of all that, the café's decor is old and the menu never changes."

"What do you suggest I do about all this?" Kelsey asked incredulously.

"Do?" Linda was surprised. "I never figured you'd do anything—not in a few short days of vacation. I was just worried you'd get the story in bits and pieces around town and go running to Clare all upset. That would make her upset and wreck your precious time together. Doesn't it seem best to just enjoy the good stuff while you're here?"

"I'm confused, Linda. Don't you think all this mess is worth fixing?"

"I'm all for fixing things, when it's possible. When somebody wants to."

"That isn't Mom."

"No, it isn't! Yet somehow, she always seems to manage. Take comfort in the fact Clare gets by and seems satisfied."

Kelsey shook her head. "I especially don't like Lewis's part in this. I'd sure like to know if he's really still trying to stick it to Mom."

"I try to keep an open mind about his intentions."

Fury bubbled forth from Kelsey. "Since when! You sure weren't confused about his motives years ago, when he fired you over a broken vase!"

"Well, since he's helped out Derek so much, I've been inclined to be a little more patient with his uppity attitude toward the hired help. It's such a relief to be able to meet him on the street with a cheery hello. And he always asks about Amy Joy. He and Bailey dote on her."

Kelsey could remember a time when she looked forward to Lewis doting on her children—his grand-children!

"I also have a new sympathy for him since the accident," Linda went on. "After losing a child, nothing can be as sweet anymore. The same with the Hansons. They've got other kids, but they can't ever be whole again. It's gotta make them a little crazier than the rest of us. At times, a little desperate."

"I'm feeling a little crazy and desperate right now myself," Kelsey admitted. "Wondering what to do about Mom, and Lewis. Wondering if it was plain stupid to come back at all."

"You've got your whole future ahead of you," Linda pointed out. "Don't let this town's troubles mess with your head. Just enjoy the reunion and be gentle with Clare. She loves you so very much."

CRAVING CLOSER CONTACT with her mother, Kelsey made a point of being in the red gingham kitchen when Clare awoke the next morning. To Kelsey's delight, Clare seemed pleasantly surprised to find her busy at the stove. And, she was still in her robe, just like Kelsey, and not about to dash out the door in that uniform of hers. For a short while, Kelsey would try to separate Clare from the café, enjoy some mother-daughter intimacy.

"Sit down, Mom. I'm making breakfast."

With a cheery smile Clare slid into a chair at one of the two pretty place settings as Kelsey came over with the carafe.

"What a treat, to be served a cup of coffee in my own peaceful kitchen."

"I've even brought out Nana's china, to really spoil us."

"I always did like to sit here and linger over the newspaper when your dad was alive. But there just isn't time for it anymore, except on Sundays."

Kelsey moved back to the stove and flipped the last

four pancakes bubbling on the griddle. Soon she and Clare were tucking into fluffy pancakes, maple syrup and assorted toppings.

"Sounds like you had some fun yesterday," Clare said smugly, as she dumped syrup on her hot and steamy stack. "According to our friendly sheriff."

Kelsey happily sipped juice, warming at the mention of Ethan. The old special energy they used to share was humming again. She was looking forward to their dance together. She asked her mother if she'd heard about that, too.

"Oh, yes. I already dug your Beauty costume out of the trunk downstairs."

"Gee, thanks, Mom, you're an angel."

Clare beamed. "It's been a long while since anyone cared enough to call me that."

"I suppose I better get my gown over to Jiffy Cleaners. I'll need it tomorrow."

"I took it to Jiffy after I closed the café last night— they're still open late on Thursdays. I ran smack into some of the other kids there doing the same." She studiously sawed into her pancakes. "So where were you?"

Debriefing, the Spy Who Wore Aqua. Getting info that should have come straight from you. Kelsey was tempted to mention the Doo-Wop, but this was meant to be a relaxing break for the two of them.

"You couldn't have been worried about me on the streets of Maple Junction!" she said instead.

"I didn't expect you were in any danger. I just wondered. That's what parents do with adult children under their roof. Wonder."

Kelsey smiled. "It's been a long while since anyone cared enough about me to *wonder*."

ETHAN PULLED UP AT THE GRAHAM house promptly at twelve in the squad car. Kelsey came right out, her auburn hair carefully styled, wearing a yellow knit top and snug beige capris, comfortable brown flats on her feet.

She rushed to the curb and yanked open the squad's passenger door with harried uncertainty. "Do I look okay?"

Ethan eyed her with pleasure. "Yeah."

"I only ask because I'm not changing between the dance rehearsal and the party at the tavern."

"You'll shine as always."

Very pleased, Kelsey climbed in beside him.

"Sarah asked that I pick them up, too," he told her, turning onto Earle Street. "So she can spend a little extra time with you."

"How nice! Time seems to be in such short supply now in Sarah's busy life."

Kelsey felt Ethan's gaze on her the minute he pulled to a stop. Sure enough, he had twisted toward her in his seat. If the twitch of his thin, neat moustache was any indication, she guessed he was nervous about something.

"I hope you don't think I'm being too pushy, but I happen to know Sarah would very much like to spend a lot more time with you."

"She has mentioned she'd like me to move home. I'm flattered she cares so much."

"Oh, she does care." He studiously traced a finger on the steering wheel. "It's likely not near as important to you, but I'd like to second her idea. I hope you give it serious consideration."

She reached over, touched his shoulder and gave him a gentle smile. "I will, Ethan, believe me."

"By the way," he said, reaching for the door handle,

"after all these years, it feels good to hear you call this place *home*."

Ethan grabbed Kelsey's hand for a relaxed stroll up the Yates walk. But the peace was short-lived.

The couple stepped over the Yates threshold to find Sarah underdressed in a huge pink shirt, her golden hair a mess as she paced the living room with a stiff and howling Amy Joy. Derek was seated on a club chair, digging through a laundry basket hoping to recycle a shirt. Sarah's mother, Isabel Matheson, who had answered the door to them, was now patiently standing by at the ironing board to press Derek's choice of outfit. He eventually inspected and sniffed a wrinkled green polo and tossed it to his mother-in-law.

"Thanks, Isy," he said, jumping up for a look at his jeans.

"The pants are fine," Isabel said, expertly smoothing the creased shirt.

Kelsey pulled Ethan to the sofa so they wouldn't be in the way.

"Mama, I fed her," Sarah lamented. "She must be sick." Pressing the child close, she whirled at Derek. "We'll never get out of here now!"

Derek cringed at their guests. "Sorry about this."

"Not a problem, Derek," Ethan soothed.

"This isn't working out at all as I hoped, Kel," Sarah lamented. "I called you over here so we could relax together."

"We'll do it another time," Kelsey assured her. "Don't worry."

"Hang on," Isabel said. "I know how to give you girls some quality time. Kelsey, you can take my salon appointment tomorrow morning at Ladies Only. You may have already seen it along Harvester, it's the old Clip Joint."

Kelsey perked up. "I did notice it, and wondered what went on behind those smoky black window shades."

"Dawn, the owner, is from Milwaukee and attended some posh cosmetology school there. She offers all the latest treatments, manicures, facials, pedicures, waxes, highlights. You'll simply love it, Kel."

"Thanks so much, Isabel."

"Kelsey," Sarah interrupted, "you and Ethan should probably go on without us."

"No," Isabel said firmly. Handing Derek his shirt, she took Amy Joy from Sarah and settled back in the big recliner for a gentle rock. "Babies fuss all the more when you fuss. Now go get ready you two, and put a smile on for Kelsey and Ethan. They must think marriage is a horrible institution."

Kelsey and Ethan were so quick to protest, Sarah and Derek erupted in laughter and the Yateses' tension burst like a bubble.

DANCE REHEARSAL AT THE GYM went well. A current student was enlisted to handle the music, while Derek managed the array of colored lights. To the pleasure of retired theater director Ann Dolan, Sarah invited her to supervise the dance number. Three couples from the original musical showed up to back Kelsey and Ethan and the group spent the next few hours relearning how to dance together.

By the end, Kelsey was convinced this bunch had no lingering misgivings about her role in the tragic accident. Just the same, she realized only those who wished her well would have signed up for the dance. The going would likely get tougher later on at the tavern when she met the rest of the class.

Chapter Seven

The Tick-Tock Tavern was a huge log cabin set in the woods off Route 7. Kelsey and Derek grabbed a ride over, as Ethan had run Sarah home to check on the baby.

She paused on the way in to enjoy the old familiar smells of pine and beer. As always the place was spotless, save for the empty peanut shells that littered the floor. The Tick-Tock was known for its free peanuts, which, Clare had once told her, were an investment as they made people thirsty. The more folks ate, the more drinks they were likely to consume. The keen entrepreneur in Clare had always liked that trick, even if she couldn't stand the thought of cleaning up all the shells at the end of the day.

Like the Cozy Home Café, the decor hadn't changed much either, Kelsey decided. But even in the low lighting, she could see the high-gloss wooden tables, chairs and booths positioned across the plank flooring were in excellent condition, unlike the café furniture. The finishing touch was the old German grandfather clock standing behind the pale wood-planked bar, providing inspiration for the tavern's name.

The place was closed to the public tonight for their

party. Like everything else about the reunion, this pre-banquet get-together had been Sarah's idea, a way to reconnect informally, circulate freely before settling down in the gym tomorrow night at their assigned seats.

To Kelsey this seemed the perfect icebreaker and she said as much to Derek now.

Pride gleamed in his dark eyes as he steered her to a couple of open stools at the bar. "Sarah is so good with people, understands how to put them at ease, get a point across with diplomacy." Checking with her first, he ordered two tap beers, included in the reunion fee.

"I'm glad you hooked up," she said, raising her frosty mug to him. "Two of my best friends becoming best of friends to each other."

He self-consciously gulped from his mug. "A toast to us sounds funny after so many years. But I guess you weren't around for any of it."

"Followed the whole thing long-distance, but it isn't quite the same, is it?" She took a sip of beer, fighting off a sinking feeling over the loss. "If only I'd known," she said brightly. "I could've played Cupid in high school."

Tough streetwise Derek, with his mother Linda's sharp tone and features suddenly looked a little lost. "Aw, Kel. That never could've worked. I was too mixed up, too un-popular. Believe me, things unfolded in the right order. By the time Sarah found me, I was ready for her, settled into running the garage, getting some respect. Back in school, she was like an untouchable princess with golden hair and soft skin, that sweet laugh." He stared off as if transported back to a Whittier High hallway. "Senior year I thought it was amazing having her locker just three doors down from mine. I never imagined actually touching her…."

Kelsey thought of lingering in the hallways with Brad on so many occasions. How things had turned upside down since then.

"You okay?" Derek asked, putting a hand on her shoulder.

"Yeah." She dabbed her mouth with a cocktail napkin.

"Funny you never found someone," Derek remarked out of nowhere.

She was taken off guard. "I will! I'm looking."

"Sorry that Tanner character didn't work out." He drained his beer and hailed the bartender for another one. "Want to talk about it?"

"Heck, no."

"You might even change your mind about him."

"Double heck no." Since when did Derek play matchmaker anyway? "Tanner was never a serious boyfriend. In fact, Derek, there has never been anyone since Brad that made me feel the way Sarah does you."

"Never?" he questioned doubtfully.

"There was a potential about three years ago—Kevin. A hot lawyer with a cool apartment in the city. But it turned out the apartment belonged to his law firm and he was a married suburbanite with two little kids." Her face hardened. "I don't know what angered me most, his intricate web of fiction or his lame excuses when I busted him. Takes a petty weak person to tell so many damaging lies, then try to rationalize it all…" Her beer was going down easier now, Kelsey discovered.

Grimacing, Derek circled his workman's hands around his second full mug. "Just want you happy. Like us."

Before Kelsey could respond, Zach Pierpont, a burly fullback from their ball team, came up on Derek's right, clapped him on the back and began to relate a woeful tale about a mysterious clattering under the hood of his Dodge truck. Kelsey smiled as she watched the exchange. Derek had finally made it all right if jocks sought his expertise. Good for him.

Kelsey slid off her stool to work the room a little. It was nerve-racking to wonder how people regarded her now, and who here might be willing to give her a break tonight. She worked her way through the room making small talk with classmates she already knew were allies, those who'd been on the reunion committee, those who'd dropped by the café. This strategy went well enough, but she could see they were distracted by friends they hadn't seen at all yet, anxious to keep on mingling.

Kelsey decided she should try the same strategy herself.

Thinking fellow cheerleaders might show some old squad loyalty, she homed in on Bridget Paulson and Diane Dwyer, standing off by the restroom door. They had checkered school careers themselves, being famous for heavy makeup, impossibly tight tops and high squeals. Always in the principal's office for copying off test papers, skipping class. Always flirting with other girls' boyfriends.

Minor infractions that made their past imperfect. Stuff they'd likely put behind them. Had they matured enough to realize she was only human, too?

The pair had been chatting until they spied Kelsey. Now they grew silent, pulling looks of disapproval. While let down, a part of her couldn't help but understand. Bridget was first cousin to Lissa Hanson and Diane had dated Todd Marshall's big brother, losing him when the family had moved after Todd's death.

Tiny ripples in the water. Sorrow over the accident affected many people.

Standing in the center of this familiar room abuzz with life, Kelsey glanced round with a jolt of panic. If only she could read minds, seek out classmates who'd accept her. As she scanned everywhere, she realized she was looking for someone in particular, the person who for so long had covered her back—her first friend, her first infatuation, Ethan.

Still finding no sign of him or Sarah, her nerves tightened.

Where could they be?

Ultimately settling for an inanimate object which couldn't give her a hard time, Kelsey made tracks for the jukebox set near the tiled dance floor. Pressing her hands on the glass surface covering the current playlist, she forced herself to be engrossed, as if it were the original Declaration of Independence miraculously touring Wisconsin.

She jumped at the pressure of fingertips on her neck. Turning to find Ethan hovering, she exhaled with relief. "Where have you been!"

"Sarah was supposed to tell you, I—"

"I know you drove her home. It just seems like you've been gone forever."

"Well, I'm back and all yours." Resting a hand on her shoulder, he leaned over her to examine the music choices on the jukebox. "What have we here?"

"Nothing much new," she marveled, running a finger down the titles. "Debbie Gibson, Sonny and Cher, Andy Williams, Beach Boys. I suppose it's hard to get forty-five platters to fit this old machine."

"Let's play something that doesn't promote jumping

around. How about 'In My Room' by the Beach Boys."
Slipping some coins into the slot, he pushed some buttons, making the speakers swell to life with guitar
strains and Brian Wilson's crooning. Without asking,
Ethan pulled Kelsey to him and began to slowly guide
her around the empty floor.

Resting his chin against her head, he pulled her more
snugly against his length. "You make me wanna dance
every time I see you."

Kelsey was warmed by the affection in his voice.
"We always were good dance partners."

"We were good together period, Kel. Our chemistry
worked right from the start."

"We did have our share of bust-ups," Kelsey reminded him.

"Considering that we grew up together, next door to
one another, I'd say our fights were pretty normal."

"We both liked to win, we both wanted to come off
as the toughest."

He smiled down on her. "How I miss it all!"

"Yeah, me, too."

The song came to an end all too soon, but the next
one, "Moon River," was also perfect for slow dancing.
Ethan showed no sign of letting her go, so Kelsey continued to follow his step.

"I remember coming here with my parents on Sunday afternoons, their only day off from the café. We'd
commandeer a booth and Mom and Dad would dance
like we are for hours. It was the only free time they had
and they wanted to maximize it."

"What did you do?"

"Great stuff. I made up new cool dances for *American Bandstand*. Drank gallons of cherry Coke, without

ice because the cold hurt my teeth, and ate candy from the machine that probably hurt my teeth more. Oh, there were the peanuts of course, as many as a stomach could hold." She shook her head. "I haven't thought of that time in ages. Mom was so alive then. She actually came here in shorts and midriff shirts. Giggled. Clung to Dad like a needy teenager."

Ethan's brows lifted. "I haven't pictured her that way in years."

"So many years ago. Dad's been dead eighteen."

"Right."

"This place hold any memories for you?" she asked as they shuffled and maneuvered with the growing crowd.

"I was a peanut-shell sweeper one summer, remember?"

"Yeah?" She struggled to picture it.

"I was only thirteen at the time so there weren't a lot of job opportunities."

"Oh, sure. You started saving for a motorbike."

He nodded. "Dad was gone so much, Mom had to handle my obsession herself. Thinking I'd never save up enough cash, she let me at it. Took two whole years of sweeping and mowing and shoveling but I finally made enough. Then found just the bike I wanted in the classifieds. Only to have hell break loose with Mom. She burst into tears, shouting about spinouts and amputations, then Dad returned early from an insurance convention to nix the whole deal."

"I remember you were pretty mad at them."

"I sure was! But only briefly. It didn't hurt my parents' case that Brad wanted a bike, too, and his parents said no based solely on the risk factor. Considering how spoiled Brad was, getting most everything he wanted, I had to look harder at the dangers the adults saw. As for Mom's broken promise, Dad told me man-to-man how hard it was for her to look after me alone when he was on the road. I'd been spouting off so much about being mature, he challenged me to prove it to her. If I did, he'd help me buy a decent car when I turned sixteen. It made more sense to me than the motorbike, so we had a quick deal."

"You did get that car right on your birthday, got your license first try that day, too. You always were a deter-mined guy who got what he wanted."

"Not always, Kelsey. Not yet, anyway."

Watching him gazing over her head, she realized he wasn't prepared to elaborate, but she suspected he most wanted to find a mate to share his life with. He probably just didn't want to admit it, after the way she'd teased him about Carol Parker.

"Moon River" segued into "I Got You, Babe." Ethan kept his grip on her and continued chatting without skip-ping more than a few beats. "Even without the car offer, Dad had gotten to me about Mom. She needed my coop-eration. You'll know exactly what I mean, with Clare having sole responsibility for you after your dad died."

"Is that why you watch out for Clare, Ethan?" she asked. "Because you know how it is for her?"

"Maybe. She's always been the spare mom-next-door, easy to like and respect."

Sonny and Cher faded into a funky Madonna song about being in trouble deep. Kelsey was grateful Ethan appeared to know when to hang it up. Steering her off the dance floor over to the bar, he asked her what she wanted to drink.

"Nothing yet. Already had a beer with Derek."

He tapped her nose. "Thought I smelled fumes on you. It's a lawman's gift. Don't even need a Breathalyzer when I pull people over on suspicion."

"Seems like cheating to squeeze the breath out of people to make the call."

"That's only necessary with certain citizens. Wait here. I have a sudden urge for a cherry Coke."

By the time he returned, Kelsey had muscled a lean-to spot by a massive log pillar.

"Wish I could land us a place to sit," Ethan apologized.

"You'd have to pull the fire alarm to do that. This is fine, really."

"So, how is it going so far?" he asked quietly, intently.

The knot in her stomach tightened a notch but she smiled anyway at his interest. "I'm doing okay. Getting a mix of smiles, glares and stares. Working the café first helped, I think. Any hard-core curiosity seekers got an eyeful over there for the price of a coffee. Though the cheaper ones settled for a peek or two through the window. Gee, has Mrs. Abernathy gotten chintzy. Almost paced a gully into the front sidewalk watching my moves each shift, but never coming inside. I was tempted to give her a coffee to go just to get rid of her."

"Maple's conscience and biggest gossip has become a penny-pincher since retiring from the electric company," he explained, not skipping a beat. "Even canceled her cable."

"So I'm a substitute for TV."

He moved his mouth near her ear. "You're streaks ahead of TV."

She tossed back her head and laughed. "This mess

I'm in is crazy! This is my home. I want to love it here again more than anything."

He eased his shoulder up off the pillar, righting himself. "Then let's go show the holdouts exactly that."

They moved into the crowd and Ethan scanned the room. "Derek and Sarah are talking to Scott and Sam Burnett. Let's start there. The twins are as funny as you remember and have lots of good stories about their car dealership. All you'll likely have to do is endure a sales pitch on some sweet buggy they have on their lot. Every old friend is subjected sooner or later."

"I'm not so sure about them, Ethan. Their mother used her *Cutler Express* column to rake me over the coals after the crash."

"You have nothing more to fear from Rebecca. While it's true she still freelances for the paper on occasion, she's no longer a tough reporter. She spends most of her days clerking at the Fashion Closet."

"You're kidding!"

"She had a change of heart a few years ago after a cancer scare. These days her main interests are writing warm human-interest stories and using her employee discount at the shop to splurge on fashionable clothes. You can trust me," he added.

She wanted to. She was trying.

Ethan proved correct about the Burnett brothers. Once Kelsey promised to take a look at a near-new Neon on the lot sometime, conversation expanded into all sorts of directions. Other classmates joined in, giving Kelsey a fresh chance.

The gathering broke up just past eleven-thirty. Pausing with Ethan to score a Milky Way bar at a candy machine near the entrance as people streamed out the door, Kelsey picked up snippets of conversation about the crowd moving over to the Doo-Wop Diner for a bite. The Hansons were keeping it open extra late just for them.

She stiffened in embarrassment as several classmates urged Ethan to join them.

"Go on, if you'd like," she urged. "It is *the* hangout these days."

He stood with arms folded. "So you know all about the place, huh?"

"Yes." With a resigned sigh she unwrapped her candy.

Derek and Sarah stopped, wondering what was up.

"We were discussing the popular Doo-Wop Diner," Kelsey explained.

The Yateses exchanged a stricken look.

"Relax. Thanks to Linda, I know all about the old Hanson deli evolving into a diner—mainly on Lewis's dime. I also know Mom ordered you not to ever tell me, because she didn't want me to worry about the competition." Kelsey shrugged resignedly. "Naturally, it's a place I don't belong, so go on ahead without me if you like."

"I'd rather Kelsey buys us each a candy bar and we take a little drive instead." Ethan smiled in appeal to the Yateses and they heartily agreed. So it was with pleasure that Kelsey pushed the appropriate number of quarters into the machine and filled their orders.

As the foursome climbed into the squad car, Ethan suggested, in a way he hoped sounded spontaneous, they stop by Shell Lake. "The water is bound to be pretty, with the moon so bright."

Derek looked hesitantly to Sarah. "In a hurry to get home?"

"No. This is just the sort of fun I had in mind for us all along."

This was all the encouragement Ethan needed. He promptly booted the ignition and wheeled out of the lot.

Shell Lake was near the Tick-Tock on Route 7 so they were there in minutes. Despite its rustic location, the immediate area offered every convenience. The well-lit parking lot they rolled into was smooth black tar with yellow parking stripes and branched off in a narrow loop of road that led to the water's edge and a boat launch. There was a picnic shelter and several tables on the grassy slope fronting the sandy beach. A circular outbuilding with restrooms and a public phone was situated closer to the road.

Piling out of the car on a burst of laughter, Ethan shushed his passengers. "I see we've got some company."

They quieted, their curious gazes following his finger. Down on the loop of road near the water, an old red Ford Tempo sat in the shadows.

"That brings back memories," Sarah murmured playfully.

So it did, Ethan silently concurred. Memories of parking in that same dark spot between the light poles tucked in the back seat of a Cutler car with some unimportant girl, while the one of his dreams snuggled with Brad in front. How he'd always wished Kelsey was with him instead. Right up until the very end.

His intention tonight was to wheel into that dark space on the pretext of viewing the lake, then steal a kiss from Kelsey. Not only would his old fantasy be fulfilled, but he could make subtle headway in showing her his feelings. So much depended upon how she responded. If she didn't enjoy it much, he could make light of it and they could move on. If she did enjoy it, he could apply a little more pressure after dropping off Derek and Sarah. He wanted nothing more than to invite her back to his place. Alone in the quiet night, they could really talk, then maybe, express themselves in other, more intimate ways.

Ethan's voice was steeped in disappointment when he spoke. "I'm surprised to find a teenager's beater parked here, so close to curfew."

"So you recognize it, too?" Derek asked.

"Ronny Henley," Ethan stated flatly. "I bet Stella Banks is along. At least she was last weekend." He glanced at his watch. "Ten to midnight. They're cutting it pretty close again, after I let them off with a warning."

"Can't you give them some leeway one more time?" Kelsey asked.

"No," he said firmly. "The town council agreed last year to boost the curfew to midnight for seventeen-year-olds. But only on the condition that the kids be home on the hour, and I issue citations to the ones who aren't." When she stomped her foot, he leveled a finger at her. "Now don't make me sorry I let you chug that second and third beer with the Burnett twins."

"You didn't look sorry when you won those bets around the bar."

Ethan chuckled. "What a pair of dummies. First Scott loses to you, then Sam steps up for the honor."

"It's all about keeping the foam to a minimum," she said on a soft burp. "I learned that at my last boyfriend's post-college kegger parties. You've got to tell the bartender to tip your glass under the spigot just right."

Sarah tugged at Ethan's arm. "I think you should roust those kids immediately. Their parents must be frantic."

"How quickly the new mother has defected to the other side!" Kelsey teased.

Ethan scowled. "I'm all for giving them a sporting chance to peel out on time. But it's going to be close. We'll go for a walk on the sand, let them see we're here. That should be enough to get them running for home."

Kelsey nudged Ethan. "They're lucky to have a sheriff who mixed things up himself as a kid and understands, unlike stern old Roger Norton."

Taking off their socks and shoes, the group trotted down to the beach and away from the Tempo. The evening was warm and so was the water. Pulling up their capris, Sarah and Kelsey waded in up to their knees. The guys stood by and watched them giggle and splash.

Ethan glanced over to a rigid-looking Derek. "Have a good time tonight?"

Not nearly as tall as Ethan, Derek had to stare up to meet his eye. But his edginess made up for his minimal height. "Just so-so."

"I heard a few guys copping free mechanic's advice off you. Bet that gets old fast."

"I don't mind, it comes with the job. My problem is, as a bad boy, I never shared the good times everybody's talking about. I don't even have great memories of this lake. Any girl I brought here was totally forgettable."

Ethan clapped him on the back. "On that, I hear ya. But it sure isn't true tonight. We've got it made, the both of us."

Derek half smiled and said nothing.

The girls charged back to the men, then the couples

walked hand in hand along the wet sand, spouting classmate gossip gleaned throughout the evening. Ethan said little, content to enjoy Kelsey, the way the moonlight shimmered on the red highlights in her hair, the graceful way she moved, the pressure of her slender fingers in his.

Best of all, she seemed to be enjoying him, too, wearing the same playful smile she'd had during their innocent flirtation, back so very long ago.

It didn't escape him, however, that Sarah and Derek had begun to check their watches every sixty seconds. He understood. The lucky pair was destined for the same bed. And, besides, they had a babysitter to send home.

They headed back in the direction of the squad car, scooping up their shoes and socks on the way. Unfortunately, the Tempo hadn't budged.

"I don't appreciate them pulling this again so soon," Ethan complained. "They seemed so convincingly sorry last week."

They all stopped abruptly near the squad car as they spotted Ronny and Stella seated on a curb. They looked so young just then to Ethan, the plump sandy-haired boy, the painfully skinny dark girl. Surprisingly, they both looked as angry as Ethan.

"Where'd you go, anyways?" Ronny whined. "We've been stranded out here an hour, waiting for help."

"We thought we were doing you a favor by ignoring you," Kelsey replied.

Ronny gave her a stupefied look. "I got in trouble last week with both our dads. They won't believe any story I tell, even if it's true." He shifted his attention to Derek. "You were supposed to fix my car last week, Mr. Yates. What happened?"

There was a weariness in Derek's tone. "When I gave you the tune up, Ronny, I warned you the car was due for a new water pump. You put it off, saying you couldn't afford one."

"You said it might be okay for a little while longer."

"There was a chance the pump had a bit more life. It could have gone either way."

Ronny tossed his hands in the air. "This is killing me! Stella's already late. I can't move my car." He glanced from one man to the other. "Can you even imagine being in this much trouble?"

Ethan and Derek exchanged a wry look.

"They've had their share of scrapes," Sarah announced.

"The priority now is to get you home," Ethan said.

Derek nodded. "Don't worry about the car tonight. I'll arrange a free tow to my garage in the morning. Richard will check to see if it is the water pump, and if it is, I'll look into finding you a cheaper reconditioned one."

"Now go collect any valuables out of the heap," Ethan instructed. "Lock it, and let's get out of here."

Ronny soon came back up the incline with an armload of CDs, a jacket and other junk to find his date in the back seat with the Yateses. Kelsey was scooted up against Ethan and had left him a spot.

"Hey, I want to sit with Stella," the boy complained.

Ethan started the engine. "No."

"I'll put her on my lap."

"My guess is she's spent enough time there already. Get in before I give you a citation." Sarah reached over the seat to hand the boy her cell phone. "Call home, give your folks a break."

Ronny wearily accepted. "Thanks, Mrs. Yates."

Suddenly Ethan felt like a cabby. Because of Amy Joy, the Yateses asked to be dropped first. Common sense told him Kelsey should be next, as he'd have to escort each kid home and offer an explanation to their parents.

But, he was determined to walk Kelsey to her door and make one more attempt to steal that kiss he was aching for.

He never had liked the Graham stoop, a concrete block with two steps cut into it. No place to hide up there, under the front light. Grasping her arm before she could take that first step, he firmly yanked her behind the closest azalea bush.

Flush against him, she gasped, her eyes dancing in the shadows. "What's all this! We doing the old hide-and-seek thing?"

"The adult version. Where nobody hides." He cupped her chin and locked his mouth to hers for a bold hot taste. She didn't resist at all. Didn't let go until he did.

Breathlessly, she placed a hand on her heart. "Hey, you've been practicing."

"So have you." Gently stroking her smooth cheek, Ethan studied her face.

The impossible dream was beginning to unfold. It just wasn't supposed to happen behind a bush. In the end, it was the sound of his own car horn, in the care of the two teens, that brought him back to his senses. "Guess this is good-night," he said halfheartedly.

"Yes, Ethan." With a sweet smile, she urged him out from behind the shrub. "Thanks, a lot. I had so much fun."

The horn honked again, making him scowl. "You'd think they'd be happy to be alone for an extra minute."

"You left one in the front seat and one in the back. What fun is that?"

He glanced back at the car. "Looks like they've gotten together in the front. I better go." He backed away, pointing a finger at her. "To be continued."

Chapter Eight

As sheriff, Ethan often got calls in the middle of the night. Both on his cell—and to the irritation of his landlady—his land line, which she insisted echoed through the building's thin walls.

Tonight it was the land line. C. Graham appeared on his caller ID. *Must be Kelsey.*

"Hey," she said in soft greeting to his pleasant baritone. "Sorry to wake you."

"I wasn't sleeping yet."

"Lying in bed though, huh?"

"I am doing that."

"Yeah. Me, too."

Adjusting pillows against the headboard, he lay on his back with the receiver at his ear. This was progress, Kelsey in bed, picturing him in bed.

She hesitated. "I wanted to say again what a nice time I had."

"It was great." Considering how unsure she'd seemed this evening, Ethan was pleased she'd phoned. Though he did sense that even now she was slightly nervous. She appeared to be leading up to saying something, taking slight pauses to clear her throat.

Under the circumstances, it didn't seem out of line to help her along. "I hated to see it all end so unceremoniously, behind a bush, to the tune of a car horn."

"It was pretty abrupt."

"But it doesn't have to end like that, Kel. I live in the small apartment building on Heron, across from the park. Unit 2-B." He sat up a little straighter. "Feel free to come over now." He tried not to sound too eager, even though he was. The very idea of holding her in his arms in private, finally chasing away any misunderstandings, seducing her openly as an adult, had become an obsession.

"Come over now?" she repeated, as if he'd suggested a trip to the moon.

"Sure, why not?"

"We've both got such a big day tomorrow. In fact, that's why I'm calling, Ethan, because I'm thinking of making it an even more important day for us."

Ethan was totally baffled now and growing a trifle wary. "How can we do that?"

"I understand that Lewis is giving a speech at the banquet."

"That's right. He's provided so much funding and news coverage to the school, the principal jumped at his suggestion." His wariness grew. He and Kelsey had just shared a fantastic kiss that knocked the wind out of anything they'd attempted as kids. They were two consenting adults, lying in bed, thinking of each other. And she was dragging Lewis in between them?

"I did come to town with the intention of having a candid chat with him and Bailey at some point," she went on, sounding a bit more defensive. "You probably guessed that, right?"

"Of course. But surely you don't want to do that at the banquet!"

"Not at all. Our business is too personal and emotional for a public place. No, I'm considering visiting them tomorrow afternoon, after my salon appointment with Sarah. I want to get it over with. Hear straight from him whether, after all these years, he still blames me for the crash, and if he's using the Doo-Wop to lure locals and tourists away from Mom's café."

"Let me get this straight," he said sharply. "You've called me in the middle of the night just to propose this—this scheme?"

"Yes. And to find out if you're willing to back me up on it. Sarah's the one who suggested you as a go-between…." Her voice trailed off now, sounding hurt.

"No, Kelsey, no!"

"Huh?"

"If nothing else, your timing is terrible."

"When would be a better time?"

Anytime, he fumed, when he was not lounging in the dark, yearning for her company, thinking by some miracle he was about to get it!

"You have to understand Lewis will be in no state to deal with you tomorrow. He's already a bundle of nerves over your visit, brooding over the fact that Brad can't be at his own reunion. I suspect he's even staying off the streets to avoid you."

"Hey, don't hold back, Ethan!"

It was more than he'd intended to say and harshly spoken, but he simply couldn't stop himself.

"I guess leaning on you of all people has been a huge mistake," she muttered in a far-off voice, as if half talking to herself.

"Kelsey, you're tired."

"Tired of being treated poorly even by my friends!"

"Kelsey—" The dial tone buzzed in his ear.

Ethan dropped the phone in his lap, his desires vaporizing like so much steam. He hated like blazes being part of this volatile triangle with Lewis and Kelsey.

Not that Ethan didn't hold out hope it could all be worked out somehow. He had put a lifetime of faith in the belief that, while brusque and controlling, Lewis was, at heart, an ethical man who seemed to soften a little with every passing year. A good idea, too, given his heart condition.

Ethan knew Lewis still simmered with rage over Kelsey's alleged role in the fatal accident. He just wasn't sure how much.

Kelsey was up against a unique challenge, to reason with an embittered man, while respecting his fragile physical state.

Ethan had always expected to be the one to explain the obstacles she would face at the Cutler mansion, to help map out a timely strategy. He had even rehearsed how a meeting with Lewis might go. Somehow, he had to get that message across to her.

He desperately wanted to phone her back. But then he remembered he couldn't with Clare asleep in the house. With her café schedule, it wouldn't be fair.

Like it or not, the call would have to wait until morning.

AT PRECISELY 9:00 A.M. Kelsey trailed Sarah into the Ladies Only Salon. True to Isabel's description, it was nothing like the old unisex Clip Joint where she'd gotten her share of perms, trims and pixies as a girl. Gone were the oatmeal textured walls, the cluttered waiting area, the claustrophobic cubicles. The space was now surfaced with mirrors and sleek black laminate, divided into three partitioned areas with curtained doorways. Over each hung a sign: Wash and Dry, Clip and Color, Wax and Polish.

Framed nude silhouettes added to gimmicky transformation that had created a feminine oasis where clearly men were not welcome. Judging by the number of black-cloaked clients already being attended to, a large number of Maple Junction women must also be sold on the concept.

Owner Dawn Bronson herself was at the shiny reception counter and Sarah was quick to make the introductions. Kelsey instantly sensed confidence in the Milwaukee transplant with her funky slanted haircut, heavy makeup and tight leopard-print dress.

"Sorry, we simply don't have anything available due to the reunion," Dawn informed Kelsey, tapping impressive talons on the counter.

"Kelsey's taking my mother's appointment," Sarah hastily explained.

"Oh." Dawn tapped a few keys on her computer, bringing up a schedule grid. "What sort of treatment have you in mind, Kelsey?"

Sarah smirked. "Something fit for a princess."

Ensconced in the Wash and Dry waiting area some minutes later, dressed in black plastic bibs, Kelsey turned on Sarah. "Did you have to make that princess crack? Dawn thought we were both crazy."

"I explained to her about the dancing."

"Beauty wasn't a princess in the fairy-tale, far as I know."

"Well, you end up with the Beast, who wore a crown, so sue me for taking creative license."

Kelsey grimaced at the mention of that particular beast and Sarah was quick to notice.

"Last night at the Tick-Tock was a lot of fun, don't you think?"

"It had its moments."

"Well, the beach was fun," Sarah pressed on.

Kelsey turned to her and smiled. "It was, Sare."

"Presumably Ethan got you home in one piece."

"Delivered me right to the stoop."

"I suppose he still had those goofy kids in the squad car."

"That he did. Kids are so cocky now. They were actually honking the horn to hurry him up!"

"And he was delayed how?" Sarah studied her with bright eyes.

Kelsey checked the room for any eavesdroppers. Nobody appeared to be listening. Three clients were seated under humming dryers reading magazines and the shampoo attendant was spraying another woman's hair with water from a noisy nozzle. "He and I… We ducked behind a shrub."

"Really?" Sarah's whole face was aglow now. "What happened back there?"

"He kissed me."

"Oh, so it's *that* way again. Interesting."

"Don't read too much into it, Sare."

"Well, there was a time when you two were more than friends."

"Yeah. Our friendship really took a hit for it, too, when those seniors came along and spirited him away. If I had never kissed him in the first place, his rejection wouldn't have mattered to me so much. We stayed friends, but the trust had gone. End of story." There had been one final chapter between Ethan and herself but even after all this time, Kelsey wasn't willing to share it with anyone.

Sarah smiled sweetly. "I think it would be safe to start kissing him again. Those tempting senior chicks are off the scene."

"If only they were the problem." Kelsey went on to relate last night's tense phone call.

They paused their conversation as the shampoo girl herded one client out and another in. Once the jet spray exploded noisily again, Sarah continued. "Maybe you woke him out of a sound sleep, despite his claim to the contrary. He might have been groggy and not thinking clearly."

"Or maybe his loyalties for Lewis run just a little deeper than any feelings he has for me. Oh, I can't believe how it hurts!" she admitted softly and with some disgust. "I stopped allowing people inside a long time ago. My number one rule is to wear a thick skin at all times."

"But isn't it fascinating that Ethan still appears exempt from the rule and can still niggle beneath that tough shell of yours?"

Kelsey's eyes grew. "*Scary* is the word that leaps to mind right now."

"I don't know for sure he really has the hots for you again, but you can rely on him, Kel. I promise you."

"Oh, you'd say anything just to get me back home."

"Yes! Or do anything. Probably even stage a whole reunion!"

"Oh, Sare, you didn't."

"Well, you were my main inspiration."

Kelsey shook her head. "You couldn't even be sure I'd come. I almost didn't."

"I ran a bit of a subliminal campaign for months to weaken you. Hit you with lots of our old photos, fond remembrances of the good old days."

"Looking back, guess I can see a pattern."

"The timing finally seemed right," Sarah gushed. "You appeared less and less content in Philadelphia, until I started to wonder if you had any dreams left at all."

How well her friend could still read her—even from a distance. "I hope I'm worth the trouble, Sare."

"And I hope *you* let go of all your doubts and worries, fall into Ethan's arms tonight and dance."

They were next up for shampooing then were whisked behind the Clip and Color curtain. Sarah greeted her usual middle-aged hairdresser and Kelsey was assigned a young stylist named Carinda. A Milwaukee transplant like the owner, with no local loyalties, she had nothing but enthusiasm for Kelsey's upcoming evening of fun. Given a description of her costume, she made several suggestions on how to style Kelsey's cap of dark hair. Forty minutes later she was sporting a dramatic sculpted wedge held solid by spray, and sprinkled with glitter to match her red highlights.

Kelsey was swiveling in the chair, admiring her reflection when a chorus of voices rose from the reception area.

"It sounds like a male sighting," Carinda commented. "Dawn's managed to make the salon so intimidatingly feminine, few men have the guts to cross the threshold."

Suddenly the curtain was whisked open and there stood Ethan, dressed in uniform blues, carrying a giant bouquet of red roses.

Kelsey shot a quick look at Sarah seated in the next chair having her buttery mane curled, to find her smirking in triumph.

"Kel! Finally!" Ethan plunged deeper into no-man's-land to present her the bouquet.

Kelsey eased out of the big black chair. "I don't know what to say."

Ethan self-consciously glanced around, as if noticing their audience for the first time. "Suddenly, I remembered how important the magical rose was to Beauty and the Beast."

"Yes. When the final petal fell off the stem, all hope was gone and you were destined to remain a beast forever."

He eyed her anxiously. "I decided not to risk that happening, so I brought over a bunch of second chances."

Her heart squeezed with joy. "Oh, Ethan."

A number of salon clients had avoided eye contact with Kelsey since her arrival, but all that had changed now that the sheriff was in the building. The cubicle overflowed with curiosity seekers, murmuring romantic aahs. Thrusting the bouquet into her arms, he put his mouth close to her ear. "I never meant to be a beast last night. All I need is a chance to explain."

She gave him a small tentative nod.

"It'll be all right. I promise." Standing straighter, he spoke in a clearer voice. "I can pick you up later. Name the time."

"I've decided to hang with Sarah until the banquet," she said quietly. "I'm helping her organize the awards and she's going to get me into my crinoline."

His gray eyes remained steadily on hers. "Well remember, I'm taking you home."

More moans of pleasure filled the room. Then Dawn appeared in the doorway, hand on hip. "C'mon now, Sheriff, I gave you three minutes. It's high time you were moseying along."

Ethan kissed Kelsey's forehead. "Until the dance."

"Until then," she replied softly.

Ethan exited to a standing ovation.

THE GYM WAS BRIGHT and humming with activity when Kelsey arrived with Sarah and Derek. Derek shot off to check the sound system. Sarah was spirited away to speak to a bartender. Kelsey went backstage to hang her frothy lemon-yellow gown, still sheathed in dry-cleaner plastic. None of the other actors seemed to be around yet. Not even Ethan, the person she longed to see the most.

In fact, she was aching to speak to him, get a clearer picture of where she stood with him. What did he feel for her? What did he want from her now? Could he actually have romantic plans for them again? The roses certainly suggested that.

It was about forty-five minutes until the program was due to start.

Standing before a full-length dressing room mirror, she smoothed the lines of her red Donna Karan sheath, reassured it was a good investment and a great morale-booster. Freshening her lipstick, she braced herself to return to the crowd assembling on the gym floor.

Whittier High's school colors of blue and gold were everywhere in streamers, bells, balloons and signs. Along the right wall was a long display of memorabilia, on the left a long bar. The center floor was full of white-topped circular tables with place settings for approximately a hundred guests. Kelsey recognized Hanson family members as they fussed with napkins and positioned glassware. Apparently the food was being provided by the Doo-Wop Diner. When Kelsey was small, the Cozy Home Café had done a lot of catering. She wondered again how much Lewis now interfered in such things.

One tragic event had caused all this trouble!

Kim appeared at her side then, complimenting her on her dramatic hairdo.

Kelsey gave her head a pat. "It's for the dance number. Normally, I prefer simpler styles."

"If you have a minute, I'd like to show you some of the memorabilia I've unearthed."

Kelsey followed Kim to the tables on the right for a closer look, and found an entire table devoted to Brad, including trophies for sports, ribbons for debating and chess, his yearbooks full of autographs and messages. Even his school passes, along with some ticket stubs, were set under glass.

Sadness gripped her.

"I believe it's a fine tribute, don't you?"

Kelsey struggled to reconnect with the present, blinking some moisture from her lashes. "Yes, Kim. It's a vivid reminder of all Brad accomplished in the short time he had."

"Is all this terribly hard for you? You must have so many private memories of him."

"After such a long time away, I have had to readjust to hearing his name, saying his name, seeing his photograph."

Kelsey picked up a framed picture of Brad and Ethan in their football gear. She remembered the occasion because the sleeve of Brad's jersey had gotten ripped.

Funny, she remembered posing for Lewis's camera along with the guys. Maybe he'd snapped more than one. She couldn't quite recall as she handed it to Kim.

Kim carefully set it back in its place on the display. "Lewis helped by providing things from his collection—like that picture."

"I'm sure he was more than happy to do so."

"He was very kind and helpful. Though sad about it, like you."

"Sadness is all he and I share these days."

"So you've never remembered what happened that night, huh?"

"No, Kim. My head injury permanently erased a block of several hours. I'd like to answer Lewis's questions—and everyone else's for that matter. But I simply can't. All I can do is keep the faith that I would never have put anyone's life in danger."

Kim patted her shoulder. "With luck he'll come to realize that. What better time to do it, as we all celebrate our past and appreciate our present? After all, the here and now is what's most important."

"Sarah and I were talking about the same thing. If only the sentiment were to catch on."

"Settled so far away in L.A., I no longer have my finger on the pulse of the town, but don't you feel if Lewis were to finally make peace with you, the others would follow?"

Kelsey smiled faintly. "Yes, Kim, I think that about sums it up."

"If it's any comfort, I put a good word in for you at the mansion."

"That was very thoughtful. I hope he didn't upset you."

"He was the one upset, but more nervous than angry." Kim shrugged in bewilderment, then impulsively gave her a hug. "I'll be leaving early tomorrow, so this might be our best chance to say goodbye."

Kelsey hugged her back, wondering how she could be making Lewis so nervous.

Kelsey made her way backstage again to find it busier. The actors reprising their roles as the Beast's household staff now mingled around in full costume while Sarah stood by the door of the ladies' room, holding the dry cleaner's bag with Beauty's yellow taffeta gown.

Kelsey took a minute to survey her friend, her lush post-pregnancy curves on display in a mint-green sundress, her long blond hair gleaming like sunshine, her fuller face pink with health. It was a portrait of fulfillment that Kelsey realized she envied.

"Where have you been?" Sarah trilled at the sight of her. "Did you even bring your underwear?"

At this point, the guys bailed.

"I have the crinoline," Kelsey assured, moving in to peel the dress free from its cover. "I stuck it up inside the gown."

"Thank heavens for that!"

"You are so fussy now," Kelsey teased.

"Just wait until you have family—it simply happens!"

More and more, Kelsey couldn't wait for it to happen to her. On impulse, she scanned the area for a glimpse of Ethan.

Sarah assessed her shrewdly. "Ethan's not back here. He wants to recreate the number just like you did it back in school, each of you gliding in from opposite sides of the stage."

"He certainly remembers everything about the production," Kelsey remarked, "right down to the roses."

"You gotta love a prince who knows the value of a tale. Now, let's change your dress and get this show on the road."

Standing stage left, resplendent in golden taffeta and chiffon, Kelsey waited nervously for the music to cue. Sarah continued to fuss over her, checking the yellow ribbon she'd fastened in her hair, smoothing the dress hem over the stiff shell of the crinoline. She finally straightened up, content with Kelsey's look. "You're ready."

Kelsey's dark brows arched. "You think. I wasn't a bit nervous over these shows back in school, but tonight I'm petrified. What if I fall over?"

"You've proven darn good at getting up again," Sarah comforted. "But it won't come to that, you'll be in Ethan's hands."

Strains of "Beauty and the Beast" swelled. And Ethan appeared from behind a curtain across the stage.

Kelsey's mouth curved in approval as she matched his stride to meet centerstage. The costume of royal-blue waistcoat, black slacks and pleated white shirt still fit him perfectly.

Slipping into his strong arms just like at the rehearsal, they began to glide and spin together. The brown mask he wore over his eyes to symbolize his beast condition was far more compelling in adulthood, adding an unexpected air of mystery.

Suddenly in her mind, he was the sexiest man alive.

Knowing she was safe in his hands, she let everything around them go—the bright lights, the backup dancers in servant costumes, the audience—and allowed him to lead.

The number ended to thunderous applause. Kelsey was sure most of it was for the popular sheriff, but she was proud of herself for keeping up her end of the show.

Ethan took her hand and pulled her backstage. They stood still together as their fellow players milled around looking for their belongings. Everyone was anxious to change into their party clothes for the banquet.

"You were fantastic!" Ethan told her. "I've always loved you in that dress!"

She glowed at his compliments but was growing tired of his half-concealed features. "Take off that mask. You are no longer a beast."

He reached up and unsnapped the brown suede strip at the back. "Really? So the roses worked?"

Kelsey grinned. "How could I stay mad after your gutsy delivery?"

"You can't imagine how gutsy it was. Guys *never* go into that female nest. Still, it was the only part of your day I was up on, so I knew I had to take the chance. But I bounced it off Monica first, and she was able to give me a sketch of the layout, so I could get my bearings."

"Well, thank you. I hated the idea of making all these plans, only to be on the outs with you at showtime."

He grasped her arms. "Look, I know I handled that call badly. Then I couldn't phone back for fear of waking Clare. But we will talk tonight. One on one. No holds barred. Any subject you like."

After reaching up to give him a quick hug, she swept off to change.

Chapter Nine

Kelsey's hands shook slightly as she and Ethan stood near their designated chairs on the gym floor, greeting well-wishers alongside the Yateses. She felt she might be regaining a few more friends. She hoped it wasn't all due to Ethan's popularity. In any case, she appreciated his steady support. Despite last night's stumble, he seemed all the more determined to be there for her.

Ethan was being distracted by several female classmates, as well as a server with orange curls carrying a salad-laden tray. Kelsey realized it had to be young Carol Parker. Plainly anxious to mark her turf with Ethan, she seemed willing to jeopardize her job with an ill-timed break.

Kelsey could understand the girl's territorial feelings. She had probably seen Ethan dancing onstage in his roguish costume. Now he looked stunning in his black suit, white shirt and green tie, and she wanted him more than ever.

Kelsey had no choice but to admit she was feeling a sense of ownership, too. Their good times together were getting so extremely good all over again.

Luckily, his stray looks her way indicated she was his main focus for the night, convincing her that springing for her chic scarlet dress, as well as the garnet necklace that set off the plunging neckline, had been a wise investment.

Finally, they took their seats at the round table. Noting that Carol had served his date a rather limp salad, Ethan frowned at the hovering girl and exchanged plates with Kelsey. Carol's expression crumpled as she flounced away with the large empty serving tray tucked under an arm.

"You take this one," Kelsey protested, attempting to return his plate.

"No, no." He was openly embarrassed now, so she shrugged and dug into the leafy greens.

"Carol still likes you very much apparently," Kelsey noted softly.

"She's young and silly and doesn't know what she wants."

"Well, if nothing else, I can't help but admire her taste in men."

His hot gaze nearly melted her.

As CHEESECAKE AND COFFEE rounded off the meal, senior-class vice president Zach Pierpont took the podium now centered on the stage in front of the purple curtain. Polite applause echoed through the gym.

"Welcome!" he said into the microphone. "It's an honor to represent Whittier's class of ninety-seven. When we voted in officers in the autumn of senior year, we all thought that president Brad Cutler would be leading us tonight." The large jock uneasily tugged at his knotted tie. "Sadly, that was not to be. But I know Brad is watching and expects us to carry on, make the best of this event. After all, he put all his energy into everything he tried...." Zach trailed off and coughed. "I will now hand off to Sarah, who will present some gag awards."

Kelsey was watching the most awkward fumble of the former football player's life so intently, she hadn't noticed Sarah sprint off. But now the blond mom was approaching the podium with a box of trophies. Hopefully the fun awards again lighten the mood before Lewis had his turn at the crowd.

Little trophies were given out to those who'd traveled farthest, had the most kids and found the most unlikely job. While these were entertaining, the more creative awards were the flashback ones. Sarah had secretly dug through records to determine who'd gotten the most detention slips, who'd taken the most sick days. And finally who'd landed the most speeding tickets.

To everyone's delight, the town sheriff won that one. Ethan accepted his prize with panache, begging his peers not to ruin his reputation by telling the town's fresh crop of teens.

Sarah then stood at the microphone beside Ethan to introduce Lewis Cutler. Lewis strode onto the stage, trying to detain Ethan, who merely smiled and moved back down to his seat beside Kelsey.

Kelsey felt his hand on her bare arm but found her attention riveted to Lewis. He'd certainly aged in the past ten years. Near sixty-five and looking every bit of it. His face was deeply grooved and his hair completely gray, barely enough left to pull off his favored pompadour. He'd lost weight, so much that his expensive dark suit appeared to hang on a hunched back and a pair of shoulder pads.

"Dearest friends," Lewis boomed into the mike, lifting his arms in an encompassing gesture. "I am so pleased to join you at this wonderful milestone in your lives. Principal Chamberlain encouraged me to say a few words to you, my favorite class.

"So many of you have stayed on in Maple Junction," he congratulated. "It keeps our community strong. Small towns often fizzle because their young people leave in search of better things. I assure you, nothing out there is more important than the sense of family we share here. Even those of you who have left and return now for a visit, will always belong to us. For all life's roads lead back home to Maple Junction."

He leaned hard against the podium now, fingers laced on the wooden ledge, eyes scanning the room. "As this is a time of remembrance, I'm confident you'll find room in your heart to remember Brad." His voice broke, but he continued with purpose. Lewis Cutler was no quitter. Everybody knew that.

"So it is with great pleasure I present to you a retrospective from my personal collection, which I call 'The Best Days of Brad.'"

There were some hushed sounds of surprise as the purple curtains opened to reveal a massive high-definition television screen, apparently set up during the meal. The lights dimmed, instrumental music sounded and the screen flickered on. And old reliable Lewis, only a bit worse for wear and with a slightly sagging pompadour, exited stage right.

Kelsey swiftly assessed it an artful little show chronicling Brad's life. There were clips of sports, parties, cars. An almost endless ribbon of snapshots of Brad every place, doing everything. With all his friends and neighbors. Except for one.

In not a single frame did Kelsey, his girlfriend, his future wife, the love of his young life, appear! It was as if she'd been totally erased from the town's tapestry!

She sat stock-still with hands clenched in her lap as the reality set in. This was sweet revenge, served up cold to her in public, at this most vulnerable moment. If nothing else, Lewis Cutler was still a brilliant innovator.

She willed herself to remain calm. The show had to be winding down as footage appeared of their graduation rehearsal, days before the crash. Brad cheerily waving at the camera. As if in farewell.

This would be the appropriate place to end it, with just enough drama to tug heartstrings, drive home Lewis's loss. Surely even this egotist had enough sensitivity to realize the remaining prom footage would be too painful for anyone to bear.

Unbelievably, the screen flickered to life again with Brad in his tuxedo. Lewis was fiddling with his son's bow tie. Bailey was holding the camera, you could hear her instructing Lewis on the knot. Kelsey remembered being there, too, offering advice but Lewis had muted her out!

How could he be so unfeeling! How could Ethan let him do it!

No wonder Ethan hadn't wanted to escort her to the mansion today. He knew Lewis wasn't about to show her any mercy, with this fiasco in the works!

All she could think of now was escape before the lights came up again. She grabbed her sequined purse from the table, slid out of her chair and scooted for the nearest exit.

KELSEY'S MAD DASH across school grounds suffered from lack of thought and direction—as well as some unsure footing. The dreamy platform sandals that looked so right with her mid-thigh dress were not made for walking, let alone running. She'd barely reached Fairfax Avenue fronting the school and was already wobbling in pain. Staring bleakly up and down the dark deserted street, she wasn't sure what to do, where to go.

She finally swung a right. The opposite direction of her mother's house on Hilton, but according to Lewis Cutler, all roads lead back home, so what the hell. Besides, she wasn't prepared to face Clare. Her mother was surely home this evening, even though, with Sundays off, it was her only night to howl. She was likely rinsing, dusting or scrubbing something, the fate of a workaholic with no social life.

Headlights appeared behind her a block down Fairfax but she trundled on, waiting for the vehicle to pass. It didn't. Rather, it slowed to a crawl. She glanced over to find a green mid-sized pickup truck, its passenger window rolled down.

"Hey!"

Ethan. She took a surprised second look at the late-model Chevy gleaming under the glow of the streetlights but kept on moving.

The truck came to stop just ahead of her. The dome light flicked on as she passed. Ethan stared plaintively out at her. "It's me!"

Fury simmered inside her. "Go away, Ethan."

"This is crazy, Kel. Get in."

"No."

"We need to talk."

"You are so out of chances!"

The truck door swung open and Ethan's feet hit the tar hard. Tearing to the sidewalk, he looked half out of his mind. He'd shucked his suit jacket and loosened the tie at his crisp white collar. His clipped brown hair was a mess, as if he'd run his hands through it one too many times.

"I understand you're upset with Lewis."

"Yes! But I'm more upset with you, Ethan, for not telling me about his little presentation."

"I didn't know! Lewis had some guys in his den the other night. They must have been putting it together at the last minute. You know how his ego works, Kel. He likely felt our Beauty and the Beast thing would take the thunder away from his speech about Brad and the table of memorabilia, so he upstaged us!"

"Of course you knew! Why else get angry when I asked you to act as go-between and take me to his house? You couldn't do that, with him hard at work hatching the video."

"No! It was your timing that made me mad."

"Right. You didn't want to disrupt Lewis's film work," she said sarcastically.

"This isn't about him, Kelsey. It's about us."

She cried in disgust. "I don't understand you. I don't understand you at all."

"Then get in the truck and let me explain."

"No."

"We had a deal about tonight." Grasping her forearm, he looked back at the rumbling Chevy, its headlights blazing, and wondered how many people were watching from the houses lining the avenue. "I'm going to talk and you're going to listen."

"And if I don't?"

He made a helpless sputtering sound. "I'll arrest you."

"On what charge?"

"Disturbing the peace."

Her gaze spun round in the emptiness. "Whose peace!"

"Mine."

Once she was settled on the bench seat beside him, Ethan wasted no time shifting into gear and rolling off into the night.

With a regal lift of her chin, she turned to stare out the passenger side. "Where are you taking me?"

"Someplace we can really be alone. Just trust me one more time, will ya?"

As Ethan wheeled onto Route 7 and picked up speed, she supposed she'd have to.

Eventually they were passing over the county line, into a wooded area she was vaguely familiar with from class hiking trips. He pulled the truck into a small clearing surrounded by evergreens, then cut the engine and headlights. The only glow was provided by a half moon, the only sound a crescendo of crickets. Turning the key as an afterthought, he quickly raised both windows. "So we won't be eaten alive by mosquitoes," he explained.

She primly laid her hands in her lap. "Just get to the point."

He shifted toward her on the bench seat, tossing his keys in a coffee holder on the dash. "You've got to believe me when I tell you I knew nothing of the video."

"I'd like to. But, Ethan, we've had our share of trust issues in the past—"

"So I got a case of senior fever in our sophomore year and neglected you."

"Yes! It was so hard for me to pretend I didn't care about that."

"You actually did care?"

"Yes!" she repeated, her voice raspier. "I let you kiss me…my first kiss. That means a lot to a girl. Our chemistry was so good, I thought it was all going to lead someplace."

He sighed. "If only I'd known. Maybe you should have given me a kick back to reality and I'd have wised up sooner."

"I was too proud. But you weren't exactly stupid, you could have figured it out on your own."

"Actually, I did. Only it was too late."

"What do you mean?"

"By Christmastime of that year, I knew I wanted you back. Then Brad had us over for his annual party and gave you that friendship band. It was the first true heartbreak of my life."

"Oh, Ethan," she gently reproved. "If only you'd said something."

"Like I was supposed to compete with Brad. You were higher than a kite over the guy."

"I suppose I was."

"Even if you'd known, the choice would have been clear. Brad Cutler was everything a girl could want. Charming, rich, fun. I understand, I enjoyed being his best friend."

"It would have been nice to have been given the choice, Ethan."

"Surely you can see how it never occurred to me at the time. Even now, I have trouble buying it."

"That isn't even the worst of it though, is it?"

"No," he conceded. "There was that final rejection."

"The truly cruel one."

"Don't be too hard on yourself, you were already hurting."

"Not me!" she squealed. "You! I left a message with your mother about the bonfire on my last night. But did you show? No! I sat out in the woods by the fire with the girls forever, waiting for you. Your mom promised to tell you."

"She did tell me. Dammit, I left you a note inviting you to the park. I didn't want to be with the girls. I wanted to be alone with you, to try and fix whatever was left between us."

"I never got that note, Ethan."

"I dropped it by the café," he insisted. "You were there, busy back in the kitchen."

"So where exactly did you leave it?"

"Near the cash register. I even put it in an envelope with your name on it, so nobody else would be tempted to read it. I waited in the park till three, Kel. I just couldn't wait anymore."

Kelsey turned to stare at him steadily through a veil of tears. "I want so much to believe you."

"You damn well better. Way too much time has been wasted." He pounded the dashboard in frustration and glared out the windshield. "All these years, I figured you'd had it with me, resented me too much for supporting the Cutlers."

"You did support them—you still do!"

"I've always been torn. I've always been on your side just as much—more. But you can't imagine how humiliated I was when you didn't respond to that note.

It was such a painful way to finish. But, I've always had feelings for you. Sarah's constant reports on how fine you were doing with the fancy education, the fancy job, the big social life really hurt."

"But I exaggerated all of that, Ethan, so the people here who still cared wouldn't worry. At last I've woken up and am trying to sort through my own confusion, figure out what to do with the rest of my life."

"And I'm not going to mess around anymore with insecurities and misunderstandings. I want to make things work with you. I want to take the good stuff we still have and build on it. And that definitely includes helping you smooth things over with Lewis."

"Then why didn't you do me the simple favor of taking me to see him when I asked?"

He sighed and rolled his eyes. "I thought you were calling about *us*, Kelsey. I thought you wanted to come over and you know…get it on."

In spite of herself, Kelsey erupted in laughter. "Oh, I see!"

"You had given me encouragement all evening. I guess I got so anxious, the sound of your voice made me a little crazy."

"All things considered, I suppose that might have been just the thing to end the evening."

"I love you, Kelsey, just as much as ever. All it took was one look at you stepping off the bus and all the happy memories started flooding back."

"I was too nervous then to think much at all. But we do have so many wonderful memories to share. Just maybe, we can start to make some new ones, too."

In response, he laid a hand on her shoulder, moving his fingers up to gently massage her taut neck.

She leaned into his touch. "Mmm… That feels so good."

"I'm hardly getting started." Holding her face in his other hand, he leaned closer to kiss her, slip his tongue between her lips. His sweet familiar taste was comforting and agitating all at once. Eager to encourage him, she braced her hands against his chest, opened her mouth wide and moved her leg over his crotch.

With a low groan he began stroking her arms, her hips, finally tugging at the zipper of her dress. She arched her back to make it easier for him.

"How careful should I be?" he huffed close to her ear.

"Uh, I'm on the pill…"

"Nice." He kissed her nose. "But I mean about the dress."

She smiled. "It's served its purpose, impressing the masses, winning the prince." She squeaked a little as he tugged the shift roughly over her hips and tossed it over his shoulder. Not once as she'd bought it, steamed it or wiggled into it, had she expected it to end up a scarlet heap in somebody's pickup truck.

Life had always been fun and spontaneous with Ethan.

Poised over her in mid-push-up position, Ethan gazed down at her slender toned body, the small sturdy bra and wispy panties only one shade pinker than her fevered skin. She looked up at him, panting gently, an eagerness flashing in her eyes. With his free hand, he made a firm broad sweep from her collarbone over her breasts, her navel, driving down into her panties. Using his fingers to pry open her moist petaled flesh, he slipped his middle finger inside her, causing her to gasp.

"Relax," he crooned close to her ear. "Let me make love to you."

She cried out softly and writhed as he firmly cupped her hair-dusted crotch, massaging her with his whole hand as he boldly and relentlessly probed her tight wet opening with that long single finger.

Even as he pleasured her, she was totally aware that her fevered response put him quickly in control of their universe. It was a moment he likely had wanted for a long while. Judging by his pleased expression, it seemed to be living up to his expectations.

"I'm going to come," she warned with a gasp. "If you want—"

"Go for it," he urged, his finger working harder and harder.

Kelsey's vaginal muscles squeezed, exploded in spasms. She closed her eyes, shuddered in release. "I never knew…"

Holding her close, Ethan stroked her hair. "All I want is you, the chance to win back your trust."

"I believe in you, Ethan," she whispered, touching his face. "You deserve it. Let's make more love, together this time."

He smiled invitingly in the shadows and reached back to loosen her bra, then slid off her panties, while Kelsey took care of all of his buttons and buckles.

With a peel of white cotton brief, he was finally naked. And rock solid.

As anxious as he was for a deeper connection on every level, Kelsey lay back flat and opened her thighs beneath him, wrapping them snugly around his hips. With a satisfied grunt he drove inside her slick passage, swelling, moving, creating delicious friction.

Slowing down, he dipped his head to suckle her breasts, stiffening her nipples, and treating her to a game of jab and retreat with his penis. Kelsey had never felt so full, so wanton. This sweet agony went on and on, Ethan displaying impressive self-control. As if he was determined to show her everything they could be together in a single night.

He drove into her with a frenzied finishing thrust, searing her, consuming her. They quivered and collapsed, their glossed skin smacking.

They retrieved their clothes from where they'd fallen and dressed unhurriedly, then sat up on the bench seat, with Kelsey cuddled in the curve of Ethan's arm.

"So, Kel, you ready to move home now?"

She patted his arm. "Rest assured the sex was that good."

He chuckled. "I really, really tried."

"And I hope we'll try again real soon. Next time, though, I'll be smart enough to recognize an invitation to your comfy bed. And will take my turn on top."

Ethan chuckled against her hair. "So my sex appeal is enough to keep you here for at least a little while then?"

Her eyes twinkled. "You have me back. We both know it. But how we'll manage to work out everything else is another matter."

They started for home. Ethan eased up on the accelerator this time to make the trip last. With the windows open, they enjoyed the cool air on their heated bodies.

"Kel, do you still remember nothing of prom night?"

Kelsey tipped her head against the truck door frame. "Kim asked me the same thing earlier and the answer is no."

"Tell me again what you do remember."

"I remember Brad picking me up, then going back to the mansion to make the video, moving on to the grand march. But that's where the images end. They don't pick up again until I'm lying in the hospital bed—with Sheriff Norton's ugly face glaring down at me. Why, Ethan?"

"I'm working on ways to figure things out. It occurs to me it might be worthwhile to reopen the case. As sheriff, I have easy access to the reports and witness statements."

She groaned.

"Sarah's always doubted the findings were fair and she could be on to something," Ethan continued. "I've been writing up official reports long enough now to understand there's an element of subjectivity involved. There could well be inconsistencies in Sheriff Norton's interpretation. But I've never looked at the original report. With you long gone, there seemed no reason to relive the pain."

"Confirming the theory that I was negligent could cause a load of fresh trouble for me with the law," Kelsey argued.

"We could take it one step at a time, see where the clues lead."

"Huh. Let's hope it isn't to jail for manslaughter."

Ethan was driving through town now, coming up on Hilton Street. "I'll leave the decision to you, Kel. We can let it go and hope most people will cut you a break. Or we do something to finally get to the truth. Even Lewis would have to respect you for that."

Kelsey cast him a doubtful look. "He could have pressed you to reopen the case himself and never did."

"That's true. But he and Norton were very close back then. He would have trusted Norton's judgment." Ethan slowed up in front of Clare's house and shifted the truck into park. "I'd like to think he'd give my findings precedence over Norton's now. Who knows where this might lead? You might finally be in Lewis's good books again."

"Perhaps the biggest payoff would be easing my own mind. Okay, go for it." She leaned over to kiss him good-night. "Don't bother to walk me to the bush."

Chapter Ten

Ethan walked over to the police station Sunday morning around ten, dressed in jeans and a forest-green T-shirt from last year's softball league. Both the station and the municipal offices along Seventh Street were closed for the day. In an emergency, everyone in town had his cell-phone number and that of his deputies, and the towns-people were basically law-abiding. If only those good people would find room in their hearts again for Kelsey.

He let himself in through the front door, wishing Monica was on duty to help him sort through the old case files. She had an amazing radar for finding things. But naturally she had a fulfilling life outside the station, the kind Ethan was struggling to build for himself.

Rooting through his top desk drawer, Ethan found the key ring for all the office locks. Flipping through the keys, he walked to the big steel door leading to the basement. After tripping the lock, he hit the lights and thundered down the stairs.

Two hours later, Ethan slammed shut yet another drawer of files and was about to roll his cushioned stool to the next cabinet, when he heard the door creak open at the top of the stairs.

"Ethan?"

His heart jumped a little. "Stay where you are! It's a dusty mess down here. I'll be up." Rising from the stool, he gave it a gentle kick to the nearest wall on his way out.

Ethan found Lewis pacing round the reception area dressed in a dove-gray suit, striped yellow shirt and navy tie, his hair styled with some kind of outdated cream that smelled vaguely like antiseptic. Most likely he'd come from church.

"Where's Bailey?" Ethan asked.

"At some meeting about the park gardens. Can a man get coffee around this place?" He stared down at Monica's desk. "Where is your girl anyway?"

"It's Sunday, Lewis." Moving to the small kitchen area across the room, Ethan began to prep the deluxe Bunn machine that produced hot drinks in a flash. Lewis had donated it, as he spent a fair amount of time visiting and preferred instant gratification whenever possible. "We are, after all, officially closed."

"Probably all for the best, as we haven't had much time alone lately."

"So happens I'm glad you caught up with me, too, Lew. Sit down, relax." Ethan gestured to the chairs against the wall. The cushions were an ugly mustard color, but comfy just the same.

Even the smallest directive tended to irk Lewis, but he looked weary and sat obediently. "I suppose you only have powdered creamer."

"Probably." Ethan checked the small fridge just to make sure. "Monica brings a fresh carton of cream in on Mondays."

"I'll take mine black then."

Ethan reached up into a cupboard to retrieve two white mugs with the town's red maple leaf logo, then stood by to watch the coffee brew.

"You vanished last night," Lewis accused.

"Yes." Ethan filled the mugs, then delivered one to Lewis with a small napkin.

"When I needed you."

"What did you need?"

"The show on Brad proved more traumatic than I expected." He covered his eyes for a moment, apparently unable to speak. He finally coughed to find his voice. "I got a little dizzy. Derek rushed Bailey and me directly over to Doc Ryder's house."

"What did Doc say?"

"That my blood pressure was sky high. When Bailey explained what I'd been up to with the presentation, he said he wasn't surprised."

"You should have known you were going too far with that prom-night footage. I imagine a lot of people were upset."

"I had to do something big to make Brad count! What with your lavish production."

"Brad certainly didn't need that size of spectacle to be remembered," Ethan insisted. "The whole thing was hurtful and unnecessary."

Lewis merely stared into his mug. "What did happen to you anyway? Bailey called and called for you over the PA system before we finally had to settle for Derek."

Ethan sighed. Derek hated like hell being his number two. Ethan wished Lewis would be a bit more diplomatic about his feelings for people. Which brought him to the subject weighing on his mind. "I was with Kelsey, Lew. She was probably the hardest hit by your program."

"She chose to return. She chose to dazzle everybody with a fairy-tale dance."

Ethan's expression softened. "I thought she was pretty dazzling, too. But I'm to blame for the dance. It was all my idea and she just went along. But she believes you were out to specifically punish her. Were you?"

"No." Lewis's scowl wavered. "I am indifferent to her now."

Ethan suspected, when it came to Kelsey, Lewis was far from indifferent. Hoping to jar those feelings free, Ethan swung a mustard chair around from the wall and straddled it, staring directly into Lewis's pale eyes. "You always said you wanted a daughter like her, pretty, with a quick wit and an interest in children. Her aspiration to be a teacher was special to you, too, as you respect teachers so much."

"No daughter of mine would ever drive carelessly. Not even a potential daughter-in-law."

"I've spent some quality time with Kelsey now and have discovered that she is still the wonderful girl you remember."

Lewis gazed between the slatted blinds on the large window facing Seventh Street. "I feel a major sales pitch coming on. What's it going to cost me?"

"Lew, Kelsey is considering a move back here."

"What!"

"Don't get your pressure up again."

"That means she'd be around. All the time."

"Yes."

"I can't bear the idea of meeting her on the street, enjoying life when Brad cannot. I fear I might explode."

"Is that why you've been staying home so much, to avoid her?"

"Yes! I thought it was just temporary. Now what will I do?"

"Let me make things better between you."

"You can't Ethan," he cautioned sharply, "so don't try any tricks, like springing her on me. She isn't on her way over here now, is she?"

"No," he scoffed. "I didn't even know you'd be dropping by." Ethan brushed some traces of basement dust from the knees of his jeans. It led right in to his next topic. "Let me tell you what I'm doing here today. I've decided it might be helpful to examine the accident with a fresh eye."

"No! If I wanted that done, I'd have asked you before. I suppose *she* put this notion in your head."

"No, Kelsey's not even sure it's a good idea."

"Oh." This surprised him. "Then she has an ounce of sense left, realizes she'll likely only end up looking worse."

"I'm gambling she'll look better," Ethan said. "It isn't easy for her, sincerely not remembering anything that happened that night, but she has decided to trust me."

"You've fallen for her," Lewis suddenly realized.

"Yes," he admitted quietly. "Again."

"So, I'm up against the birds and the bees. This was a big secret to keep from me, Ethan. After the deep loyalty we've shared."

"It wasn't a secret. I didn't know how I felt until I saw her again. You're finding things out almost as they happen." Ethan studied his hands, measuring his words. "I've never let you down, Lew. You can continue to count on me."

"You will, however, carry on with this probe despite my objection."

He nodded. "Yes. I love you, Lew, but I love Kelsey, too. The invitation is always open for you to share our joy."

Plainly offended by the idea, Lewis stood. "Just know before you start digging that your good intentions could backfire on her."

"But things can't possibly improve for her without better closure. Kelsey wants her good name back. She especially needs it if she hopes to land a job at the elementary school."

"There is no vacancy at the moment."

"You know full well that Mrs. Brown would like to retire if a suitable candidate came along to replace her."

"Mrs. Brown's got plenty of zip left," Lewis countered. "She's good for a couple more years."

"If she had the choice," Ethan maintained, "she'd retire."

"I am thinking of you in all this as well, Ethan. If you found my prom footage painful, just wait until you start thrashing up accident-scene photos and accounts. They're graphic and tragic. You may even come to resent Kelsey just a bit yourself, become leery and frustrated of her supposed memory loss." He tapped the side his head. "She might believe Roger Norton and I were tough on her, but it was horribly aggravating, wondering what sequence of events were locked up in her brain."

"Nothing will stop my inquiry," Ethan insisted. "It's the reason I was in the basement searching the file cabinets when you got here."

Lewis stretched out a hand, his eyes narrowing. "I demand to see what you found."

Ethan held up empty hands. "I haven't found anything. Yet."

"Oh." He completely deflated then.

"You should go home now and rest. I imagine Doc prescribed some medicine to help."

"Yes, yes he did." Lewis trudged out the door.

Ethan glanced out the window to see two cars brake as Lewis jaywalked across Seventh Street.

KELSEY WANTED TO LET THE PEOPLE closest to her in on her immediate plans, so she invited them to her mother's house mid-afternoon.

Sarah arrived carrying Amy Joy, with Derek close behind schlepping some belongings left at the gym last night, the Beauty and the Beast costumes and Kelsey's carry-all bag. Ethan arrived soon after, toting the gourmet ice cream and sugar cones Kelsey had asked him to pick up at the drugstore.

The moment they got comfortable out back on the patio with their cones, Sarah started in with the questions.

"So, Kel, are you all right?"

Kelsey glanced at Ethan and smiled. "Everything is fine. Naturally, I was upset over Lewis's grandstanding but Ethan came after me and we…arrived at some understandings."

Sarah pursed her lips, visibly impressed. "You had a busy day, Ethan, first the roses, then the rescue."

"All worthwhile, as I've managed to convince Kelsey to stay on, at least for a while."

"Hurray!" Sarah clapped her hands. "Did you two celebrate behind the bush again?"

Derek glanced around at the trio. "Suddenly I feel out of the loop."

Ethan rolled his eyes. "Your wife wonders if I kissed Kelsey and I am happy to say I did. It was all very nice by the way, Sarah, in case you're wondering."

"Which we know she is," Derek put in, chomping hungrily through his cone.

At that moment Clare appeared at the open kitchen door. "You didn't tell me there'd be ice cream at the party," she chided merrily. "I would have hurried Teddy through our errands." She called Teddy to tell him to bring them each a cone, then took a chair at the table under the umbrella beside Sarah and the baby. "So what were you saying, Ethan? You kissed Kelsey behind the bush? I imagine you mean the azalea out front. You always did like to kiss her there. At least during that cute little time you dated."

Kelsey grew a self-conscious pink. "Mom, please."

Clare shrugged. "I thought it was cute."

"Cute or not, we're officially dating again, Clare," Ethan announced.

"But Kelsey doesn't even live here!"

"Mom, if you'd slow up and let me explain."

With the slap of leather flip-flops, Teddy bounced out of the house with two towering cones. "Hello, everyone!"

Clare took an ice cream from him. "Sit down, Ted. Kelsey's gathered us for a reason. Maybe many reasons."

Kelsey took a breath and stood. "We were discussing the news that I intend to stay a few weeks."

"Here in town?"

"Yes, Mom. With you, if that's okay."

"I suppose that's fine. You can probably use a rest."

"I'm not after a rest," Kelsey said. "Now if you'll just listen. I want to live in Maple Junction for a time to decide if a permanent move back is possible."

Clare twisted in her chair to confront her daughter, unaware of the ice cream dripping down her hand. "But what of your wonderful life in Philadelphia? The career and friends you have there?"

Kelsey handed her mother a napkin from the table. "It's true I do like my job. But all my college friends have scattered and have new interests."

"You have that lovely friend, Marta."

"Marta's great but we have little in common. She's older and has a husband and teenagers to look after." Kelsey paced and bit her lip. "To be totally honest, things in Philly were never quite as great as I led you to believe."

Clare was flabbergasted. "You pretended to be happy?"

"Well, yes, to ease your mind. Just like you maintained the café was still going gangbusters to ease mine. When all the while you had some stiff competition in the Doo-Wop Diner."

"Oh, I am handling the Doo-Wop just fine."

Kelsey wasn't going to argue that point right now. "Anyway, I've decided the way I've been living isn't cutting it. I'm ten years out of high school and none of my dreams have been fulfilled. While I probably will never know what happened the night of the accident, I've decided I deserve some happiness. So, I'm going to have a second look at some of those old dreams and see if I can make them come true."

Clare had been stroking the baby's cheek and now stiffened to give her hovering daughter her full attention. "How can you ever hope to make things work for you in Maple Junction, dear?"

"I don't know yet, Mom! Can't you just be happy for me trying?"

"Are you saying you no longer wish to teach? But it's your true vocation."

"She could teach here, too, Clare," Sarah asserted. "Mrs. Brown, the second-grade teacher, would like to retire."

"Bailey Cutler runs the elementary school board almost single-handed," Clare pointed out. "Does anybody here really think she's about to give Kelsey a job?"

Kelsey slowly twirled to find a bunch of hanging heads concentrating on their ice creams. Except for Ethan. His cone was all gone and he was dying to speak.

"Clare, I admit that if asked today, Bailey likely wouldn't help Kelsey. But I have a plan that might help mend fences with the Cutlers."

Clare regarded him in sheer disbelief.

"I intend to take a new look at the accident. Who knows? Maybe I'll see something nobody else did, manage to raise doubts as to Kelsey's culpability."

Grooves of worry appeared on Clare's forehead. "And what if that fails, Ethan? What if your digging only makes matters worse?"

"Those are fair concerns. There is the chance that any new findings might put a further strain on Kelsey's reputation, not that it will get her into trouble with the law, because I would never let that happen."

"But with more damning evidence, she definitely wouldn't be welcome here even for the odd visit," Clare fretted.

"There is that risk," Ethan conceded with a measure of concern. "But since Kelsey and I have discussed it, I've come up with an idea. It makes sense that Norton used every possible angle against her the first time. Which could mean any details that didn't support his theory were deliberately pushed aside. There must be a few and I intend to find them."

Kelsey touched Clare's shoulder. "Ethan is right on. The Cutlers and their supporters will need to believe in a new version of the crash to ever cut me some slack. As I can't remember what happened, it will have to come through another means."

Openly troubled, Teddy appealed to Ethan. "I wonder what Lewis will make of this inquiry."

"Ethan thinks he'll respect me for the effort," Kelsey assured him. When Ethan didn't respond, she focused on him. "Right?"

"He came by the station this morning and it turns out he isn't too crazy about the idea."

"Oh, no."

"At this point, he has no interest in dealing with you at all."

Kelsey put her face in her hands.

"Please don't panic, Kel. He's not well. Derek had to rush him to the doc last night."

Derek nodded. "A fact that should be giving you second thoughts about messing with his nerves right now, Ethan."

"It was his own video that did him in, Derek."

"But your dance fired him up in the first place. If you ask me, I say give him a break and let the accident lie."

"If you ask me, Derek," Sarah spouted, "I say you humor the coot way too much."

Clare must have sensed tempers might spiral out of control for she stood and raised her calm no-nonsense voice. "I think we've got the general picture. Naturally you and Ethan have a right to test your ideas. Of course I want you back, Kelsey. Just the same, I think you should take this slow, make sure you don't throw away one dream before finding another. In other words, don't give up your Philly job just yet. Now if any of you would like to stay for dinner, I'm making my not-so-famous-but-tasty lasagna."

Derek Yates was swift to decline, using the baby as an excuse. Sarah looked a bit huffy as she followed his lead. Feeling guilty, Kelsey sensed an argument in their future.

IT WAS DARK WHEN KELSEY WALKED Ethan out to his truck at the curb. Pausing on the boulevard, he looked over at his old family house, a rambler similar to the Grahams' with yellow wood siding in place of their white stucco.

"Is it strange to think of someone else in your child-hood home?" Kelsey asked. "Do you have to fight the sentimental memories?"

"I pass by here quite often, so I've gotten used to it."

"Of course," she said sheepishly. "It would feel ordinary to you by now."

"I'm not saying I never feel a loss, but there are lots of fun times to think back on. Between our families, the two of us."

Kelsey's eyes rounded in excitement. "Remember the Fourth of July we climbed up onto your roof for a better view of the fireworks?"

"I was grounded for a week," he retorted. "Not because of the deed itself, but because I dragged you up there with me. Dad chewed me out good. Turns out a gentleman doesn't take a lady on the roof—for any reason!"

"Mom actually had a real live date that night," Kelsey recalled with awe. "Came home late and never found out. Boy, did I have a time concocting a fake reason for you being out of the picture for seven whole days!"

"Serving the time had to be worse," he insisted.

"So, you feeling risky again?" she asked saucily. "Like to spark some fireworks of our own?"

His eyes gleamed with interest. "What do you have in mind?"

"I could take a walk to your place later and show you."

He leaned against the trunk of a giant elm, his mouth crooked in amusement. "You carefree teachers with summers off. I have laws to enforce first thing tomorrow!"

"Oh, I'll be working at the café bright and early myself. There must be some task Mom'll let me do."

He gazed up at the sky, still playing it cool. "Guess it's okay. If you don't put too much pressure on me."

"Said I'd be on top next time." She flicked his chin. "Now go home and get excited."

He lurched from the tree with a small salute. "Already halfway there."

An hour later a nude Kelsey was sliding with a seductive purr between the sheets and over Ethan's spread-eagled body. He growled long and low in return. The possibilities were endless on this wide comfortable mattress compared to the confining truck seat. Sensations so much easier to explore. She took her time grazing her soft body against his hair-roughened length, testing the friction. Then using her tongue and fingernails, she flicked him, teased him, licked him.

Finally, she sat over his erection and rode him until they both fell limp with exhaustion.

In time she popped out of bed and moved to the lamplight to pull on the black sweats she'd chosen for the jog to their nocturnal rendezvous.

Ethan rolled on his side to watch her. "Come back anytime."

"I intend to do that often."

Ethan sobered a little. "Your mother was right this afternoon, about you not giving up your day job just yet. You always dreamed of teaching, and should make sure you can continue to pursue it one way or the other. I'm not necessarily glued to this town."

"Don't worry, I want to stay right here. The job comes second to that."

"Just know there's wiggle room."

Fully dressed, she moved to the mirror on his dresser to rearrange her dark mop. "By the way, what's with Derek's theatrics this afternoon over the decisions we've been making? I know he's tied snugly to Lewis, but he was acting like some sort of hyper Cutler watchdog."

"With you in the mix, I think Derek finally sees the chance to upstage me with the old man, prove that he can better look after his interests. All along Derek has imagined he and I have some serious rivalry going on for the top spot with Lewis. I'd gladly step aside for him, but Lewis's pretensions make Derek's struggle impossible. My modest middle-class background and stable parents make me acceptable, but Derek's rockier start with abusive, drunk Chet Yates will never quite cut it."

"Poor Derek."

Ethan balked. "Old Derek is doing fine with a lovely child and a pretty wife. I'm the lonely bachelor with the empty bed."

Touched by his forlorn look, Kelsey stripped off her top with a sigh. "Okay, show me some of that wiggle room you were bragging about."

Chapter Eleven

The café had just a handful of customers Monday morning when Kelsey showed up at eight to a less-than-enthusiastic welcome from Clare and Linda. By the time her mother pulled her aside around eleven, she had a good idea of what was coming.

"We simply don't need you."

"Ouch! Slide in the dagger."

Clare rolled her eyes. "Knock it off, Kel. I've been giving you hints since you got back. While I appreciate your willingness to help, this place can't sustain another full-time waitress."

Kelsey shuffled her comfortable shoes. "I guess not."

"Why don't you take my earlier suggestion and rest up? You deserve some downtime after a challenging school year."

"I'd be bored to tears."

Clare snapped her fingers. "I knew it! After years in the city, I knew you'd find this place a snooze."

"Hey, I know." Kelsey impulsively grabbed Clare's arm. "I'll take *your* place for a bit, so you can have a rest."

Clare gaped. "Excuse me!"

"Go shopping for shoes, a dress. Get a brow or bikini wax, maybe."

Clare's laughter pealed. "Only floors are waxed in Maple Junction."

Judging from Clare's ancient hairdo, Kelsey figured she still had it cut by old Mrs. Bergerson in her basement, and had never set foot in Ladies Only. Now she suggested a trip to the salon, to get the works, her treat.

"Really, Kel, I don't need any of that Molly coddling. Now be a good girl, hang up your apron and scat."

Kelsey surrendered in a huff. Of course, Clare didn't really *need* any of the pampering Kelsey had proposed. What she needed was a batch of new customers, but that seemed as unlikely to happen as the wax job.

By mid-afternoon, Kelsey was sitting on a park bench facing Second Street and the Doo-Wop Diner. She'd gone home, changed into an orange tank top and navy shorts, looked in on night owl Uncle Teddy still slumbering noisily, then had eaten an energy bar in front of the TV. Normally active every waking hour, she couldn't stand being cooped up anymore and had taken off for an aimless stroll.

Or perhaps this spot in the park had been her true destination.

Last night, after leaving Ethan's Heron Avenue apartment, she had detoured up Second Street for her first close look at the Doo-Wop. Pausing at the big window pane, she'd cupped her hands against the glass and peered inside. In the faint glow of the security night-lights, she'd discovered a fifties wonderland on a checkerboard floor. An old-time soda fountain in lime, yellow and white with big swivel stools, spacious booths and round tables with cushy seats. The center-piece was a huge retro jukebox of gleaming chrome and colorful glass tubing. All in tip-top condition by the looks of it, even after ten years of service.

It stung her to think Lewis might still be helping the Hansons with ads, civic catering jobs and mentions in tourist brochures. Clare's business sorely needed a boost and, as a town leader on so many local commit-tees and boards, it seemed only right Lewis should dole out the perks more fairly.

But on the other hand, Clare's could do more to draw in customers, make an effort to compete for some of the town's business.

Suddenly inspired, Kelsey abruptly shot up from the bench. The bottom line was that Clare needed to re-charge her business, to open her mind to growth and creativity, to revitalize the café.

In other words, it was time to intervene.

ETHAN WAS SLIDING A TICKET under the windshield wip-er of a shiny maroon Suburban parked next to a fire hy-drant on Fifth Street when Kelsey charged up to him and touched his back.

He turned and smiled. "I dropped by the café for lunch expecting to see you. Heard you were canned."

"I'm still a standby temp—at least I hope so. So have you found the file on the accident yet?"

"No. Monica says reports dating back that far got shipped to the library basement before old Norton retired. Apparently they're stuffed in boxes in no particular order."

"That seems stupid and careless."

"Or contrived. Norton was such a self-righteous

autocrat. I figure he didn't want his cases handy for re-evaluation or possible second-guessing."

"He always did have an ego."

"I'll get over to the library soon," Ethan assured. "The minute I'm free."

"Holler if you need help."

Worry creased his forehead. "I suppose you're bored sick already."

"I did mope on a park bench for a while over near the Doo-Wop Diner. But then I got an idea. There is no reason why Mom can't improve her business, crank up the competition a notch."

"A suggestion she's sure to hate."

"I'm thinking of more than a simple mention. Rather, an intervention."

"Kelsey…" The lines on his brow deepened. "Such a strong-armed move will only make her angry. After ten years apart, do you really want to do that?"

Kelsey expelled a breath and paced a little on the sidewalk. "I've always known she never got over the deaths of those kids. We've always been good at feeding off one another's guilt, but I never visualized her life quite as bleak as it is. With all the hours she's put in at the café, she should have a lot more to show for it, more customers, more profits, more staff, more downtime."

"Kelsey, you don't know anything about small-business makeovers and the Hansons aren't about to tell you how they rose from their modest deli beginnings."

"True. But the Ladies Only salon is another example of an amazing turnaround. Owner Dawn Bronson came out of nowhere to transform an old-fashioned place like Mom's into a trendy money machine. She was friendly enough when I went in there Saturday, so I'm confident she'll be willing to give me tips to get us started." She stood on her toes to kiss his jaw. "So if you need me in the next hour or two, you'll probably find me at the salon."

Ethan shuddered loose a deep breath. "Oh, no, you're on your own in there."

THE OFFICIAL LAUNCH of Kelsey's plan was set for Tuesday evening, just after closing time.

Linda greeted Kelsey and Ethan when they walked through the front door at eight-fifty. "Clare's already suspicious."

Kelsey gaped at her. "Why?"

"Because I'm lingering longer than usual. And," she added reluctantly, "because I smoked more today and messed up a few orders."

Kelsey was exasperated. "You're supposed to be upbeat about this."

"When I know she hates change?"

"Maybe she doesn't hate it that much." Kelsey sounded more hopeful than she felt.

"Anybody with an eighties hairdo in the twenty-first century despises it. I tried to warn you in the park about interfering, remember?"

Linda closed her mouth as Clare appeared then from the back room, her aqua uniform wrinkled, her tried-and-true hairstyle limp.

"What's up?"

Before Kelsey could respond, the front door opened again. And again. Soon the café was filled with everyone on Kelsey's support-group list. She turned to lock the door and swing the sign hanging on it to Closed.

A spooked Clare, now demanded to know what was going on.

Kelsey wound an arm around her mother's small shoulders. "We want to talk to you about sprucing this place up, making some real money around here."

"You are kidding. After the long, tiring day I've had?"

"If you had short days, I would've picked one of those."

Clare watched Ethan and Derek push a couple tables together and gather chairs for everyone. "How big is this plan?"

"Pretty big," Kelsey enthused. "A café makeover."

Clare looked stunned. "I knew when you got bored you'd start to pick on my life. You couldn't rest a mere forty-eight hours."

"Like mother, like daughter." Kelsey parked Clare in a chair and dropped down beside her. Everyone else followed suit, except Linda hovering in efficient waitress mode.

"Lemonade and cookies?" Receiving nods all around, Linda hustled off.

"Keep going, Linda," Clare called out. "Right out the delivery door."

"Mom!" Kelsey scolded.

Clare rubbed her eyes. "Let's get this over with."

Kelsey made her pitch with gusto, drawing on her discussion with Dawn. Like the old salon, the café was rundown, stuck in a rut. Comparing haircuts with food made sense, too, as people looked for variety. Theme places currently worked well in all sorts of businesses. Dawn had exploited the idea that her place was too exotic for men, but naturally, Clare wouldn't want to go that route.

"Change is expensive," Clare stated simply. "That counts me out. It always has."

"So have you considered change in the past, Mom?" Kelsey asked.

"At times, I guess. Then I'd do some math, look at my calendar, and forget about it."

"Let's not look at the expense for a minute," Ethan suggested.

"He's right," Teddy chimed in. "You can't see a dream clearly when it's hiding behind a dollar sign."

"Look at me," Derek invited. "I started with nothing and look at my business now. It can happen."

"I don't expect Lewis Cutler will be subsidizing me!" Clare sniffed, then paused. "That was uncalled for. Derek, you helped him the night of the crash and got rewarded for it. Our family…played a different role."

"Mom, we can't help that those kids are gone," Kelsey said, her voice shaking a little.

"All three of them such good kids, who spent happy hours right here."

"Yes, wonderful friends who would never expect a grudge to spill over on you, and wouldn't want you to feel guilty about having a bigger dream. Can we please try to let go of that sadness?"

Clare nervously wet her lips. "I guess it can't hurt to talk about new ideas, a new theme."

Ideas flew for the next ninety minutes. A Trekkie eatery with orders dispatched via two-way radio. A romantic grotto with a waterfall. A disco-mania café with a constant dance beat and a glitter ball spinning overhead. A big-top carnival look.

"How about an ethnic slant?" Teddy ultimately blurted between bites of yet another cookie. The crowd grew silent, expectant. He excitedly brushed the crumbs from his mouth. "Italian? Chinese? I mean, you're all so worried about competing with the Doo-Wop's decor. Seems to me that the food should be the most important thing."

Kelsey reached over and clapped his pudgy cheeks. "Brilliant! Mom does make great pasta sauce from scratch!"

"This is promising," Ethan agreed. "People have so little to choose from here in town. There's the little Chinese takeout across from the station, but there is no Italian within fifteen miles."

Kelsey stood and perused the room. "It wouldn't cost nearly as much to redecorate this place in Italian style."

Clare remained wary. "But it won't be cheap either."

"I'm the one pushing this, Mom, so I'll find the money. I have some savings, and we can get a loan from the bank using my condo as collateral."

"I can get a crew in to gut—I mean, remove your old fixtures," Ethan offered.

"I can wallpaper," Sarah announced. "Linda can, too."

Clare looked around, a trifle lost. "Paul and I did all this together. What would he think?"

"He liked change," Teddy reminded her.

"Dad did have a fun, daring streak, Mom," Kelsey insisted. "You always loved that about him."

"The risk factor could be scaled down," Ethan proposed kindly. "You could phase this in gradually, if you think that's best. Begin by replacing the furniture and fixtures with neutral red-and-white pieces. Any accessories could wait until after you've introduced a few Italian dishes, maybe just at dinnertime. Breakfast and lunch could stay the same while you see if the Italian fare takes off."

"We could start off by presenting it buffet style," Linda suggested. "To let people try different things."

"And just where will all this food come from?" Clare fretted. "Artie can't do it all. Turning that mailman into a fry cook was one thing…"

"The changes should pull in bigger profits. Some of which could be used to hire more people to lighten the load, shorten the shifts. C'mon, Mom, let's show this town we've still got it!"

"Oh, all right. Let's do it!" Clare finally relented, beginning to glow. "But I'm not changing the name. Paul wanted Cozy Home and that's forever."

"So the question is, how soon can we close you down? The sooner the better—"

"What are you talking about, Kelsey?" Clare asked.

"The remodelers need to get in here, Mom."

"All at once?"

"It would be best," Ethan agreed. "I did some construction in college so I know what's involved. There are builders in Madison who can do it for a reasonable price."

"How long will it take?"

"Oh, ten to fourteen days."

"Closed for two weeks!" Clare was appalled.

"You can do some of those things I suggested yesterday," Kelsey teased.

Clare reddened. "Like hair removal? Ridiculous!"

"The guys need the space and freedom to work," Ethan said patiently. "They won't have it if you're open, and I doubt they'd take the job. But you won't be resting. You'll be home working on your new recipes, the menu, your ad campaign. Then you can re-open with a bang—with the Italian dinnertime buffet." Ethan took a short breath. "What do you think, Clare? I can make some calls tomorrow."

Clare's mouth took on a shy grin. "Okay. Get an estimate."

"And I'll sketch out some ideas," Kelsey announced. "So you can get a feel for what you want, Mom."

"Are you sure about the money, Kelsey?"

"Out of your hands," she insisted.

After the group dispersed, Kelsey and Ethan strolled along Harvester, his arm draped over her shoulder.

"You should feel pretty good right now," he remarked.

"Everyone deserves family support. And Mom's gone without for way too long. Now all I have to do is cough up the money. I'm sure not looking forward to facing Sidney Strom at the bank tomorrow to bare my assets, put myself at his mercy. There's just something about that guy I don't like. He's so…slick."

"You do remember Lewis is a majority owner of the bank, don't you?"

"I remember. With any luck he won't have a chance to interfere before I get some kind of assurance from Strom."

"I want to be there with you tomorrow, if that's okay."

"Oh, Ethan, you just keep on saying all the right things."

"How does 'will you come home with me now,' sound?"

"Right again."

Holding hands they crossed Harvester Avenue and took a shortcut through the dark park.

ETHAN MET KELSEY at the Maple Junction Savings and Loan early the next morning. He completed his uniform with his gun and a tie, not sure how else to look sober, responsible and a bit intimidating. Kelsey had taken special care with her appearance, too, donning a cream suit jacket and skirt and pale blue blouse. Her hair was combed away from her face, secured with a gold headband. Her high cheekbones and vivid green eyes were barely tinted with color. The effect was elegant, appealing and capable. He vaguely wondered how many first-grade boys had crushes on her each year.

As soon as he saw them, the bank president was scooting out of his glass office. Sidney Strom was a stout round-faced man of fifty-nine who talked in rapid-fire sentences. It seemed handling the town's finances was a heavy burden.

"Anything the matter, Ethan?" he demanded nervously.

"Gee, no, Sid." Ethan didn't like the pretentious little snot any more than Kelsey did but smiled at him anyway.

"I have a business matter to discuss with you, Sid," Kelsey announced.

Without a word he ushered them into his office.

Strom politely listened to Kelsey's pitch, though his eyes kept glancing up to the ceiling. As if, Ethan thought with annoyance, he was silently begging to be beamed up to the mother ship. Not too off base, as he was a *Star Trek* enthusiast. Maybe they should have gone with the science-fiction theme for the café after all.

"Small-business loans are risky," Strom announced pompously.

"Put up against my condo?"

"I've already spoken to a crew of able workers," Ethan

smoothly lied. "It won't even take that much capital." He threw an estimate at him.

"But you need to make a profit in order to pay any amount back," Strom protested. "Who will come to the café to eat this Italian food?"

"Pasta lovers?" Kelsey challenged.

"Young woman, I think it will take a bit more than a love of pasta to solve your mother's problem."

Kelsey grimaced. "So who did you lose in the crash, Mr. Strom?"

He actually looked surprised. "Nobody. This is a business decision. You would struggle to lure customers to the café. I would struggle to keep the ones I have. Those who, as you say, lost someone in the crash."

"Where would the customers go, Sid? You're the only game in town!"

"Now, Ethan, the bank's image must always be my first concern."

Kelsey stood. "Well, give my regards to Lewis the next time you see him."

Following a hunch, Kelsey paused out on the street to peer through the bank window. Sure enough, Lewis was now in the glass inner office with Strom.

"I have half a mind to go back in there."

"Please don't, Kel. I'm not pleased with Lewis myself right now, but confronting him at the wrong time will only make matters much worse."

"I'm growing sick of his tactics."

"With good reason."

"I won't let him hide behind his heart condition forever."

"Nor should you. But to take a run at him this way when your emotions are running wild will put you at a disadvantage. Likely you wouldn't get your point across in the best way."

"Fine. Let's get out of here."

Ethan suggested they take a moment together on the bus bench before he went on to the station.

Kelsey took off her headband and shook her hair into a mussed cloud. "It appears somebody at our private meeting squealed to Lewis. Who'd do that?!"

Ethan reached over to gently rearrange her hair. "Don't jump to conclusions. Lewis showing up might be a coincidence."

"You have to wonder if we have a spy though. It could be Linda, she seemed all over the map about Lewis when I spoke to her that night in the park."

"Maybe it's Derek. I told you how anxious he is to please. No matter, I don't think we should dwell on it. We need our energies to keep going, work on swinging those funds."

"You still have hope?"

"A lot of hope. First, I'm going to make good my lie at the bank, confer with the builders I know. I'll compare prices to the assets you revealed to Strom and see how much more money we need. Meanwhile, you sketch out those plans for the remodeling, something we can give a pro to start on."

"What should I tell Mom?"

"Avoid her for now—at least till the end of the day. If she learns the loan fell through she'll see it as an excuse to back out."

"Suppose I could slip home and change, collect some sketch supplies, then go hide out at the library."

"Perfect. We'll meet at the station about five."

ETHAN WAS LATE GETTING BACK to the station for his meeting with Kelsey. It was nearly six when he marched into the reception area through the back way. He surprised both Kelsey, flipping through a magazine, and the night deputy, Chuck, seated at Monica's desk, ordering chow mein from the little take-out place.

Kelsey dropped her *Redbook* and rushed over. "You okay? Chuck said you got an urgent call."

"I'm fine." He glanced over at Chuck. "Fred Bellamy is cuffed out in the squad. Go help Nate haul him down to lockup. Then head for the hospital to take his wife's statement. She's scared enough to press charges this time." Once Chuck dashed off, Ethan gave Kelsey's arms a squeeze. "The Bellamy boy is all grown up and acting just like his daddy did."

Kelsey sighed. "That's too bad. I used to babysit him."

"I'm pressed for time, so just listen. I talked to my old friend Jason Frye and he's available to start work on the café. As I figured, we can keep costs down by closing it up and helping out with the teardown."

"Even then the bid can't be low enough to avoid a loan, Ethan."

"We can avoid a loan by pooling our savings—the two of us, I mean."

"Did you have that in mind all along?"

He nodded. "Think of the huge advantage, having total control without bank interference."

"Mom won't want you taking the risk."

"So don't tell her. But she trusts you, she trusts me. It'll be swell, you'll see."

"Oh, Ethan. I don't know…." Despite her hesitation, she was pleased.

"Jason is meeting us at the café at 6:00 a.m. tomorrow for a look around. Unless I call to cancel."

A door slammed in back and foul language erupted. Smacking her tight little tush in neat white shorts, Ethan urged Kesley toward the door. "I'd like to give you time to raise a feeble protest, but I'm busy. Go tell Clare we're set."

She stared up at him affectionately. "You are amazing."

"You can tell her that, too."

IT WAS AROUND 10:00 P.M. when Ethan sat down with a leg up on his desk to peruse Chuck's statement from the hospital. He skimmed the details and cringed. It was high time for Heather Bellamy to press charges. Swinging his foot to the floor, he sat upright to rifle through the stack of papers left by Monica earlier on. A worn yellowed file folder caught his immediate attention. He pulled it forward and read her attached Post-it note: *Had some free time. Dug this out of the library.*

It was the file. Labeled Cutler Accident. Unexpectedly featherlight for such a weighty occurrence.

Heart pounding, he leaned back again in his chair, his feet atop the desk. And began to read.

Single-car accident on sharp bend along Route 6 at Prine's apple orchard. A 1995 VW Jetta slammed into tree, ejecting all four passengers. (Names, ages, addresses above.) Skid marks and tire tracks obscured by heavy rains. Hydroplaning suspected, also due to rain. Cutler and Hanson died at scene, transported to Maple County Hospital for autopsy. Marshall and Graham transported to County for treatment. Impact forced engine into front seat. Graham handbag found shoved down front seat driver's side, Hanson shoes in back. Contents of glove box: tissues, compass, flashlight. Contents of trunk: jack, spare tire.

Ethan studied the enclosed diagram that showed where the victims and their possessions had fallen. Lissa Hanson and Todd Marshall had been found on opposite sides at the rear of the car. Brad and Kelsey had been found near the front driver's side.

Ethan's heart slowed and sank. Nothing here seemed to rescue Kelsey's reputation. It only boosted Lewis Cutler's position, that Brad had indeed crawled around the car to reach Kelsey. Bleeding internally, it could well have been his last, deadly decision.

Tossing the file across his desk, Ethan rubbed his eyes. All this time, he'd held out the unrealistic hope that somehow Kelsey hadn't been behind the wheel. But she'd been closest to the driver's door and her purse had been wedged next to the seat.

How was he ever going to tell her?

Chapter Twelve

Ethan and Jason Frye arrived at the café at six to find the Graham women waiting with big smiles. Ethan made the introductions. Jason fit the image of a friendly lumberjack, a big, tall redhead with an easy personality.

"My hero." Clare reached for Ethan and hugged him. "Kelsey told me."

"Are you okay with it?" he inquired.

"I am concerned about paying you kids back, but it sure beats answering to Sidney Strom. He is such a pompous man."

Kelsey laughed along with Ethan, wondering if her mother had had dealings with Strom in recent years. It occurred to her that she knew nothing of Clare's financial situation beyond her obvious frugal lifestyle.

The foursome spent time discussing Kelsey's sketches and poring over Jason's catalogs. He took notes, gave them a reasonable quote and promised to return in a few days with a crew to start the ripping-out phase. The whole project would be complete in two weeks if the new equipment arrived on time.

Clare showed her gratitude by having Artie whip

up a superb pancake feast for them when the café opened at seven.

After Jason left, Ethan asked Kelsey to join him on the sidewalk.

"What's up?"

"We need to talk privately."

"Oh?" She raised her brows. "A little afternoon delight at your place?"

He slipped on his sunglasses. "My place is a good idea. Say about two?"

"Hey, you know me. Jobless and available." She grew furtive. "I could go over to the library now and search for that mystery file for you. If it wouldn't be stretching policy too much."

"Uh, that won't be necessary."

"So you have it."

He attempted a smile. "See you at two."

Ethan made a point of having some of her favorite soda, cherry Coke, at the apartment, but Kelsey hardly touched it as she reread the report in his small living room that afternoon. "I'm tempted to say, I told you so, Ethan."

Towering over the old floral sofa where she sat, he anxiously raked his clipped hair. "Maybe I should have let things be. I just held out a vague hope…"

"Of what! That I wasn't there at all? That I have an evil twin? Well, I've long given up on that sort of dream rescue." She shoved the file back at him.

He weighed it in his hands for the umpteenth time. "This thing feels so light," he complained. "It barely reflects the tragedy, the lives lost, Sheriff Norton's method of reporting, Lewis's demanding nature."

"It's enough to bury any goodwill left out there for me."

He sank beside her on the sofa and stroked her cheek. "Sorry."

She set her half-empty glass on an end table. "Can we agree to finally let this go?"

"Sure."

"Nobody else should care enough to make a fuss," she mused. "As you said, Lewis didn't want the issue reopened at all."

"True. He did demand to see the file on Sunday, though, when he thought I'd found it in the basement. Don't worry," he hastily added. "I'll bury this thing again myself. In my personal stash."

Her forehead creased. "Let me get this straight. He wanted to stop you digging, but at the same time, he wanted to know if you found anything."

"Yes. He keeps alluding to the idea that you returned with an ulterior motive."

"Why didn't you mention this to me sooner?"

"Because I hoped to figure out what he was talking about first. But it's become clear he's never going to tell me. The way things stand, he still wants to ask all the questions without giving any answers in return."

She flipped her hands in the air. "Well, I'm speechless. There is nothing to his suspicion. Nothing."

THE NEXT TWO WEEKS WERE a whirl of activity. The Graham kitchen was a testing ground for Clare's Italian dishes. Linda and Artie spent hours with her, experimenting with different recipes. Kelsey and Ethan worked with Jason and his men, gutting the café. They were deliberately mysterious about what they were up to, hoping to create a buzz around town that wouldn't cost them a dime.

Some sort of advertisement would be needed soon, however, as Jason's work drew to a close. It was Ethan who first broached the subject at the Graham table while they taste-tested a rich mushroom sauce over pasta.

"Kel, a clever campaign has to include an ad in the *Cutler Express*," he insisted, twirling noodles round his fork.

"I couldn't agree more," Clare chimed in.

"But you loved my colorful flyer idea."

"We need both." Hands on hips, Clare regarded her daughter. "You may as well accept that we'll have to deal with Lewis in the long run. It won't be so bad. He and I have learned to get on, truly. I'll go to the newspaper myself tomorrow to place the ad. It won't be big like the Doo-Wop's, mind you, but it will be nice. I'll use the money Aunt Grace sent me for my birthday."

"It would be even better if they sent a reporter over to interview you about the new look," Ethan proposed. "That would be extra free publicity."

Clare snapped her fingers. "Yes!"

"Let me arrange that," he offered. "Rebecca Burnett will do a good job."

Watching Ethan and Clare eagerly plot on, Kelsey wanted to believe the newspaper would come through, that Lewis hadn't stopped the loan. She even wanted to believe the reunion video of Brad was just a father's sentimental whim gone wrong.

She wanted to have faith in all those things to energize her, give her the strength to eventually face the Cutlers and make peace with them. But for now that goal still seemed unreachable.

On a warm evening in late July, the group that had been called together to brainstorm ideas to refresh the café were called back to view the final results. Teddy arrived first, affecting a regal air that was supposed to match his gig clothes, a plum suit and black shirt. Linda came next, after crushing a cigarette on the sidewalk. Sarah and Derek followed, pushing Amy Joy in her buggy.

Kelsey stood back with Clare and Ethan, watching everyone walk in and look round in wonder. Tiffany-style lamps suspended from a pristine white ceiling replaced tin fixtures and water-stained ceiling tiles. Red-and-white checkered flooring buffed to a high gloss lay in place of the cracked tan linoleum. New cherry-colored furniture stood where tattered orange stools and chairs used to be. And gleaming gray granite topped the old chipped Formica lunch counter and tables. This last provided at cost by Jason Frye's father, a ceramic dealer, who thought Ethan was okay.

And Mr. Frye wasn't alone in his view, Kelsey thought.

So much had happened since her return. She'd fallen back in with Ethan so easily, she was beginning to find life without him impossible to imagine and was growing restless to make a more formal commitment. Diamonds, she thought wistfully, were always a good symbol of formality.

"There are a few tasks left to do in the kitchen," Clare announced, "but we hope to open in two days' time."

Applause and cheers filled the room. Then the door opened again. Rebecca Burnett, reporter/salesclerk appeared and her jaw dropped a mile at the sight of the makeover. Kelsey's mouth opened just as far at the sight of Rebecca's own makeover. The woman she remembered as drab and heavyset was now a petite, strawberry blonde dressed in Anne Klein! Presumably, spending time at the Fashion Closet had inspired her.

Rebecca excitedly opened her tote to extract some cute rainbow-framed reading glasses and a steno notebook and pen. "I believe I've got myself a scoop! So somebody start talking." Everyone did. All at once.

The grand opening was set for Thursday afternoon at four, featuring a buffet of their Italian recipes. So it was early that morning when Kelsey picked up a few copies of the *Cutler Express* at the drugstore and walked down Harvester to join her mother at the café. She arrived expecting to discover Clare and Linda hard at work. Instead, they were glumly seated at the new lunch counter, the newspaper carelessly spread out before them.

"What's wrong?" Kelsey demanded, taking the open swivel seat between them.

Clare, her elbows propped on the granite top, merely rubbed her face. Linda lashed out, however. "The ad here is a quarter of the size it should be! And it's buried on the sports page next to an article on next winter's plans for a kiddie broomball team!"

Leaning over, Kelsey moved Linda's finger off the page to study the small printed square. "Why, it's only about the size of a short obituary!"

"May as well be one for all it's worth," Clare sputtered.

"What about Rebecca's article?" Kelsey asked.

"She dropped by a few minutes ago," Linda said miserably. "She swears she got it to the newspaper on time."

"I only hope this was a true misunderstanding," Clare said bleakly.

How could her mother be so naive? Lewis had done this on purpose. With a huff of indignation, Kelsey got up, went over to a brand-new aluminum trash bin and shoved her copies of the newspaper inside.

Clare watched her worriedly. "What's on your mind?"

Kelsey rounded the counter and pulled a stack of red paper off a shelf underneath. "I'm going to deliver these flyers to every business on Harvester."

"Ethan already did that."

"I'll pretend I didn't know it. At least I can see how many got posted." With that she flung out the door. She was back within thirty seconds though, looking sheepish. "Guess most places aren't open yet, are they?"

That gave the three cause to laugh and relieved some of the tension.

When Uncle Teddy made the mistake of stopping in for breakfast around nine, Kelsey reminded him they wouldn't be serving breakfast until tomorrow, after the grand opening. Then used a dose of charm to quickly enlist him to take the flyers down the avenue.

Meanwhile, Kelsey, Clare and Artie toiled in the newly equipped kitchen while Sarah and Linda set up the buffet table out front.

Ethan showed up about three-thirty. "I'm sorry about the ad and the article, but I've talked up the buffet today as much as I could."

"We've done our best to get the word out," Linda shouted through the order hatch.

"Well, put me to work," Ethan invited. "I'm yours for the night."

Kelsey grinned, imagining quite another meaning to his words.

At four o'clock, all was ready and the women were dressed in their new red uniforms with crisp white collars and candy-stripe aprons. With great ceremony, Clare went to the door, turned the sign on the window from Closed to Open, and bowed.

Customers began to trickle in. Jason Frye's jolly construction crew escorted attractive dates. Monica Blair showed up with her boyfriend, hardware store owner Mr. Hinkie, and her cousin Loretta Evensen. Sarah and Derek arrived with Sarah's parents Isabel and John. Abigail Forester and Danielle Slade brought a few fellow teachers from the high school. The largest group was led by Rebecca Burnett. She was so sorry about the article snafu that she was treating her sons Scott and Sam, along with their families and a few of the regular customers at their car dealership.

Kelsey propped the front door ajar on the warm summer evening, allowing laughter to drift into the avenue, and the ploy drew in some extra patrons.

By eight o'clock, however, the place was empty again. A big disappointment, as they'd intended to run strong until at least nine. It got even worse when Clare added up the receipts.

"Taking into account wages and food, we didn't come close to breaking even," she reported, sinking wearily into a seat next to her helpers.

No one dared to mention the money put into the remodeling plus Clare's loss of two weeks of regular business.

"This place should have been packed!" Ethan thundered in disbelief. "Everything looks so wonderful…"

"It was all a big risk from the start," Clare reminded them.

"It could have worked, if Lewis had just stepped back

and done nothing. But he couldn't resist shrinking the ad and sinking the article. And we can only guess how many people stayed away to support him." Kelsey bit her lip, simmering with anger. "The worst part is, he stays in hiding while he ruins us!" Unable to handle their sad faces, she spun on her heel and headed for the door. "I need some fresh air."

Ethan joined her as she leaned against the building. "Anything I can do?"

She met his eyes. "Drive me over to the Cutlers'."

"We agreed you were going to be in control for that visit."

"Ethan, he's gone too far." She climbed into the squad car parked at the curb and poked her head out the window. "I simply can't take any more."

Ethan's pulse jumped at his throat as he slowly drove out to the Cutlers' country estate. Reaching the dirt road marked Cutler Trail, he parked. "I can't let you blindly rip into him. I insist we discuss what you are going to say."

She folded her arms, thinking hard. The rumble of the car engine was the only sound for some minutes. "I'm not sure. I've rehearsed so many speeches. At this point, none of them seem adequate."

"If I can offer you some advice, Kel?"

"Please do."

"When you first got here you talked about wanting to get beyond the past and moving on. I think that is exactly what Lewis needs to do, too."

"Has he ever shown you a sign that he is interested in doing that?"

"Well, no. But perhaps you can show him the way. If it's any comfort at all, I sense that deep down Lewis still has feelings for you. He just can't seem to separate those feelings from his anger over the crash. I know you can't apologize for what you don't remember doing, but maybe if you can convince him you share a common pain over losing Brad, your rift can heal and he can stop holding you totally responsible."

"Okay, Ethan, I'll try it that way. Let's drive on and do this."

The cool, blond lady of the manor answered Ethan's ring. "Oh," was all she could say at the sight of him with Kelsey.

"May we come in, Bailey?" Ethan asked.

"Lewis is tired," she warned but she opened the door wider.

Bailey led them to the den where Lewis was resting in his recliner, watching a nature program on TV. Wearing a robe over pajamas, his hair disheveled, he looked spent.

"We have visitors," Bailey announced, moving to switch off the set.

His wife's dull tone obviously didn't prepare Lewis for the sight of Kelsey. He was thrown completely off balance, his eyes wide, his mouth sagging.

"You! You come to my house uninvited?" He gripped the arms of his chair and glared at Ethan. "You, boy, knew I didn't want this!"

"Give her a chance, Lew," Ethan pleaded.

"We need to talk," Kelsey insisted.

Lewis grunted. "Young lady, our business is long over."

"How can you say that after today's fresh bag of tricks?"

Lewis was momentarily startled. "You must be referring to the mix-up over the newspaper coverage. Well, one of the *Express* staffers thought he was doing me a favor when he acted on his own."

"The thing is, it's just the kind of favor he was sure you'd like."

"Well…"

"Whether you take action against us yourself, or have others do it for you, it doesn't matter. You are ultimately responsible. Shame on you for keeping it up ten long years."

"That's nonsense."

"Really? You continue to help Mom's competition clean up with civic catering jobs, advertising and blurbs in tourist brochures."

"Your mother has always been free to compete," he groused.

"When I finally convince her she's a worthy opponent, you stall our loan at the bank!"

Lewis reddened in discomfort.

"Furthermore, you make Ethan feel like a traitor for showing me kindness. You play a video of Brad's last day that squeezed the joy out of the whole reunion and reminded people that you think I'm horrible."

He pounded the chair arm. "That video was necessary to make the kids remember. That's what I hate most, Kelsey, the idea that Brad might somehow be forgotten—by you and everybody else!"

"Nobody is going to forget Brad, Lewis, least of all me."

"But you've moved on to a nice life. You're respected, admired. I hate that you got off so easy."

"Easy, huh?" Kelsey paced around the opulent room. "Funny, it all seemed terribly hard. I was barely eighteen when I was tossed into the world on a blast of your rage. Feeling shaky, guilty and insecure, I was forced to carry on alone. I struggled to support myself, make new friends I felt I didn't deserve."

Her voice grew hoarse. "My life was destroyed in an instant by that crash. I lost my whole future with Brad, you and Bailey. And I couldn't even remember doing anything wrong. I've never been a reckless or uncaring person, Lewis. Whatever happened wasn't a deliberate act." She shook her head at their imperious expressions. "Does nothing reach you? I loved your son with all my heart! Losing him wrecked everything. Everything!" She broke off with a sob.

In response to Lewis's moan, Bailey rushed to kneel by his chair, stroke his thinning white hair.

Ethan stood by, speechless.

Then suddenly Lewis clutched his chest and slumped. Bailey instantly jumped to her feet and lunged for a button on the desk intercom. "Ethan, we better call an ambulance."

"Right." Ethan grabbed for the phone beside the intercom and punched in 911.

It was now where Ethan's loyalties would always lie—squarely with Lewis Cutler. The fury inside her now churned out of control. What a fool she was to trust him again! She wondered all of a sudden if he'd ever written her that note the night before she'd left for college. Or if he'd merely made the story up to seduce her. Maybe it was another case of the bored sheriff captivated by the new talent in town—Carol Parker all over again.

Carol Parker herself appeared in the doorway then, summoned by the button.

"Carol," Bailey said, "escort Kelsey Graham home immediately. You needn't come back afterward."

The young redhead smirked. "I'll get my purse, ma'am."

Kelsey held her bubbling dismay in check as Carol drove to Hilton Street in her old Chevy. The minute the car's taillights were winking in the distance, Kelsey set out running, all the way to the old Hawkins place on Earle. She pounded on the front door with both hands. When a befuddled Derek answered dressed in tattered gray sweatpants and T-shirt, she flung herself into his arms.

"I think I killed him! Lewis!"

Sarah rushed into the living room as Derek was bracing up Kelsey and kicking the door shut. "What's wrong?"

"She finally snapped, Sare," Derek yelped. Holding Kelsey away from him, he searched her face. "You shoot him or what?"

Kelsey slapped his shoulder. "Idiot! I only talked to him. Suddenly Lewis was clutching his chest, Ethan was calling an ambulance… What have I done?"

"Ethan should have known better in the first place," Sarah scoffed.

"I made him take me there. It was a horrible mistake! Everything's ruined."

"Don't panic, we don't know the old man's dead yet."

Derek began to pace. "I should be at the hospital, too. What if he dies and I'm not there?"

Kelsey knew about Derek's devotion to Lewis but was startled to see it played out. Before the accident had made Derek a hero, their paths had only crossed through Sheriff Norton whenever Derek had cut a Cutler car off with his illegal motorbike.

"Derek, you're tired. You have to work tomorrow." Sarah clutched his arm. "You've been trying to break away from him," she whispered with feeling. "Let Ethan and Bailey handle this."

Derek swayed against her. "You're right, hon."

Sarah turned to Kelsey with a bolstering smile.

"If Ethan doesn't call here, we can call the hospital. In the meantime, let's sit down and wait."

Derek trudged toward the kitchen. "Kelsey, you want a beer or a wine cooler?"

"You choose for me. I don't have another decision in me tonight."

Derek called at midnight. Word was that Lewis had indeed had a mild heart attack but he was sedated and resting comfortably. Kelsey went home to bed.

ETHAN WAS SHAKEN AWAKE by a nurse the next morning. Like Bailey, he'd stayed the night at the hospital.

"Good morning, Sheriff."

"Good morning." He sat up, still fully dressed in yesterday's pants and polo. All he'd removed were his shoes. "Is he awake?"

"Oh, my yes. The doctor has released him and Mrs. Cutler is signing the papers." She handed Ethan his shoes. "Mr. Cutler certainly has power and influence, doesn't he? Your concern is especially touching. He says he regards you as a son. So nice," she cooed, "since his real son died."

"I've been around since way back," Ethan admitted, noting a hundred-dollar bill in her white uniform pocket. He suspected she was flying high on a Cutler tip.

"I was on duty the night of the accident," she confided. "Awful thing. The poor little girl who lived was like a scared little bird. Is she all right now?"

"I hope so." Ethan's heart thumped heavily as he recalled the look in Kelsey's huge green eyes as Bailey had thrown her out. It had all gone so wrong. But, at the time, he was being pulled in too many directions.

"Different sheriff then, of course," the nurse was saying. "But just as respectful to Mr. Cutler, followed his every order. Just like we did."

Ethan tuned back in with a blink. "Did what?"

"Followed Mr. Cutler's every order. Back then."

"What kind of orders? His son was already dead."

She scowled slightly. "Oh, nothing, really."

Bailey pushed open the door then, looking tired but relieved. "We're ready when you are, Ethan."

AFTER TWO WEEKS OF HEADING over to the café with her mother first thing every morning to help with the renovation, Kelsey awoke to find Clare had gone on ahead, no doubt to finally reopen for breakfast.

Kelsey didn't want to interfere, but couldn't help worrying. What if after a two-week gap, her regulars had found somewhere new for coffee and pancakes? She had to find out.

Dressed in her uniform, Kelsey entered the café through the delivery door to make a discreet assessment of the situation. Artie was at the grill as usual, merrily preparing eggs and bacon. Peeking out the swinging door, she discovered some of the old patrons scattered about. Clare was circling with a water pitcher but zoomed back to the lunch counter at the sight of Kelsey and pushed her into the kitchen.

"What are you doing here?"

Clare's hard tone stung. "I got in the habit of helping you, is all."

"I know about last night," Clare proclaimed. "Everyone does."

Who'd spread the word so fast...? Of course, Carol Parker, still smarting over Ethan's indifference. "I can explain, Mom."

"Unnecessary."

"Okay, but—"

"It's not okay by any means," Clare spouted. "I've been getting along fine all this time—"

"You mean until I returned to spoil things?" Kelsey cut in shrilly.

"Kelsey, Ethan hasn't been in. I think he's angry too."

"He went to the hospital."

"The word is, Lewis is already home."

"I see."

Clare shook her head with a frown. "Is it true you managed to upset them all?"

"I bet that's Carol Parker's version."

"She's one source, but I spoke to Bailey today."

"Since when do you two share confidences?"

"I had to call her. I feel so responsible for Lewis's... episode."

"But you're not!"

"I am, through you. Bailey told me Ethan can't stop apologizing for taking you over there."

Kelsey's heart squeezed painfully. Could Ethan do that to her, knowing how Bailey would use the information? No matter what loyalty he felt for Lewis, he wouldn't, would he? "I'm sure she exaggerates."

"It doesn't matter in the long run. Everybody always believes the Cutlers."

"I am so sorry if I upset your life."

"That's the main thing, Kelsey, it *is* my life. I've settled for it."

"You deserve more, though, Mom!"

"Well, look around. I listened to you and now I'm more behind than ever, and have new worries about paying you and Ethan back."

"I don't care about the money. I only care about us." Unable to hold back the tears, Kelsey ran out the way she'd come.

Chapter Thirteen

Kelsey returned home and like in the old days, poured out her heart to Sarah on the kitchen phone. Like babbling teenagers, they rehashed everything, down to a detailed replay of what Kelsey had said at the Cutlers'.

"I don't feel comfortable calling Ethan, Sare. His loyalties obviously are trapped forever in that musty old museum. As if that's not enough, Mom is devastated. I don't see any choice but to cut my losses and go back to Philadelphia." Turning to find Teddy at the counter getting coffee, she cut short her conversation and hung up. "I suppose you got an earful."

"Yes. I do realize it's none of my business, though."

She waved. "Oh, it's all in the family. Even a dysfunctional one like ours."

"Ah, we're not so bad." Pouring two cups of coffee, he invited her to the table. "Come sit and I'll give *you* an earful."

"Uncle Teddy, I'm not up to another lecture."

He tsked. "That isn't my style. No, dear, I want to explain why you can't run off feeling a failure."

"But I am one!"

He gestured to an empty chair. "Sit."

"All right." She sank next to him and took the extra mug.

"As you suspected, the café hasn't been doing too well. In fact, it has been doing a slow, steady *Titanic*-like sink for quite some time. Clare's put up the fight of her life, as you can imagine, waving from the deck, listening to the band, pretending to the town she isn't drowning at all."

"I think I understand her determination The food business is all she really knows."

"That's right. I've pitched in with funds whenever I've been able. Finally, I sold your Nana's house to give her all that cash. It's helped keep her afloat for a while. But the truth is, she was about to go under for good when you showed up with your renovation idea. It was a welcome last chance."

"But nobody caught the Italian wave."

"The locals didn't come in droves as we hoped. But many people like Italian food and I believe they'll try it soon enough. And the new interior will attract more tourists. It's all for the best. As long as you and Ethan can wait for payback."

"You should have told me sooner, Uncle Teddy, given me the chance to help."

"I figured it was wrong to force you back after you had the courage to rebuild your broken life. It was best to let you return when you were ready."

She shrugged. "Maybe you're right."

They sipped their coffee in companionable silence.

"You planning to see Ethan today?" he finally asked.

"Probably not. If you heard even half my call to Sarah, you know why." She walked over to the counter to refill her mug. "I think it's fair to say he isn't too anxious to see me right now, either. I do realize we're both to blame," she added, returning to the table. "I forced him to drive me to the Cutlers'. He dumped me when Lewis collapsed. All I wanted at the end was a smidgen of support from him, but when all I got was a stony stare, I knew for sure that even now he can't stay loyal to me under pressure. I wonder if I should ever have trusted him again."

"Once he calms down there's a strong possibility you will hear from him."

"Oh, I'm not banking on it."

"It could be as soon as today."

"What are you driving at, Teddy?"

"I'd rather not say. I did after all, hear about only part of last night's adventures." He stood and went to set his mug in the sink. "Just don't turn him away if he comes calling, Kelsey. Give him a chance to explain himself."

Just as Teddy had predicted, Ethan caught up with her later in the day. She was walking down Harvester Avenue carrying a sack of toiletries from the drugstore.

He slowed the squad car down to a crawl. The passenger window was open, and she could hear him clearly. "Kel! Can we talk? Please?"

She paused on the sidewalk, still aching over his coldness last night. Then on impulse, she gave in and slipped into the front seat of the car.

"Great!" Beaming, Ethan accelerated down the avenue.

Within minutes he was pulling into the parking lot fronting the lake. He switched off the engine and shifted closer to her. "Sorry about the way things spiraled last night."

"It's okay, Ethan," she said cooly. "I'm glad Lewis survived. It wasn't my intention to kill him. Please tell him that for me."

"Will you stop being so formal? I know you want to shout, kick up a fuss."

She glared at him. "Well, you were sort of a jerk, Ethan! All I wanted from you was some sign of support before I left. It was horrible, riding home with smug Carol, listening to her clucking. I can't help but wonder if you deserved my trust after all and always cared the way you said." Her voice broke a little and she turned away from him to stare out the windshield.

"You probably even wonder if I really wrote that note."

"Well…yes."

Ethan reached over her then to open the glove box. He extracted a stained yellow envelope. "I found this during the café renovation. It had slipped between the counter and the cash register."

She stared at the yellowed square of paper wedged between his fingers. "It's *the* note?"

"Yes. Would you like to read it?"

"Have you read it?"

"Not since I wrote it. I'm sure it's a painful, mushy mess, full of clumsy language." He shook his head. "I think I even offered to run away with you."

"Oh, Ethan!" She sighed, pushing the hand holding the envelope away. "I don't want to read it now, like it's a piece of evidence in a dispute. Maybe someday, we can read it together."

Tossing the note back in the glove box, he reached out for her. "I love you so much, Kelsey. I'd die if I lost you all over again."

"Then what happened last night? I realize you were

under pressure, but to completely block me out was awful."

"It's kind of tough to explain."

"Is it that complicated?"

"It's downright simple, really, just sort of humiliating." He hesitated. "I got jealous of Brad all over again."

"Ethan, he's gone."

"That's part of the problem. Your perfect teen romance is frozen in time. I panicked when you went on and on with such grand passion about how great Brad was, how much he meant to you. I was swept back to the days when I felt so inadequate, felt I could never hope to steal you away from him."

"It was your idea I express those feelings, try and bond with Lewis."

"That's the most humiliating part! I brought the whole thing on myself. When Lewis had the heart attack, I knew I had to shut you out to concentrate on helping him. I admit, I was also pretty angry with you. I was hoping I'd ignite that intoxicating level of passion in you myself."

"If it's any consolation, I lost control because of you. Lewis disgusts me so much I'm only trying to make things work with him for your sake. Just the same, I never should have doubted your loyalty. I promise it won't happen again."

Seeking his mouth, Kelsey gave him a sample of that impressive passion.

They decided to take a walk on the beach. The afternoon's wind gusts had tapered off, making the sun's heat warmer on their skin. Barefoot, sunglasses shielding their eyes, they strolled hand-in-hand close to the lapping water.

Kelsey told him about her run-in with Clare, and Teddy's account of her mom's financial woes.

Ethan listened with interest. "I'd like to think we've done the right thing with our investment, and Teddy probably has a point about the Italian angle catching on."

They continued to stroll, making small talk. Kelsey tried to relax but she was sure Ethan still had something on his mind. Back at the car, she asked him what it was. He paused near a picnic table and sat on it. Rubbing his hands together, then briefly over his jaw, he surveyed her from behind his dark lenses. "I want to ask you something. I have no right to, and it might make you mad."

"Gee, fire away," she invited wryly.

"Did you and Brad…ever have sex? I know it's a lot to ask," he added. "But after what you said about him last night, I keep picturing all kinds of things. I'm sure the images will go away. Someday."

With hands on hips, Kelsey rocked before him on the table's cool concrete slab. The question was personal and nervy. On the other hand, she was sure he'd suffered enough.

"No. He wanted to do it, like most teenage boys. He kept a box of condoms in his glove box, in hopes I'd weaken one night. But he was fine with waiting, even kept his sense of humor about it. I thought it was pretty good self-control, considering he got his way with most things in life."

Ethan smiled in relief. "Thanks. While it wouldn't have mattered all that much if you had, it somehow means the world that you didn't. That you don't hold that particular cherished memory along with the others."

Kelsey stepped between his legs, knelt on the table's bench seat and put her arms around him. "At best, it would've been two kids fumbling around. Nothing like us..." She snuggled close, kissing his face, nipping his ear.

"There are some advantages to being an adult," he rumbled. "Knowing how to do things right."

"Let's go back to your place for some of that grown-up fun."

ETHAN FIGURED HE'D HAVE no trouble falling asleep when Kelsey left around 2:00 a.m. After last night in the hospital and all the commotion today, he was exhausted. But something had been niggling the corner of his mind all evening. He just couldn't tune it in. He shut his eyes in the dark and lay perfectly still.

Then he remembered. Brad had kept a stash of condoms in his Jetta's glove box, Kelsey had said. But they weren't listed in the accident report. So what had happened to them? Could be he'd given them away. Lost track of them. That didn't sound like his old buddy Brad. He'd always been coy about any sexual relationship with Kelsey and had always kept that glove box locked.

Ethan closed his eyes. It probably meant nothing.

KELSEY AWOKE EARLY SATURDAY to the aroma of breakfast. Curious, she grabbed her robe and ambled out to the kitchen.

Clare and Teddy were seated at the table, eating. Kelsey could hardly believe it—the plastic rooster clock on the wall said almost eight! Late for her mother, early for her uncle.

"Linda's opening for me," Clare explained.

Kelsey sank into a chair. "Thank God, I thought you'd closed down!"

"Oh, Kelsey!" Clare chided.

"We needed a quick family meeting to set things straight before they could fester," Teddy announced. "I've spoken to Clare about our talk, Kelsey. She—"

"Let me," Clare cut in. "Honey, I'm sorry I've given you a hard time, hidden the fact that I've been in such dire straights. Your efforts at the café have made a difference. I don't know if I'll be able to hang on to it, but I'll give it the best shot ever. At least, it's now attractive enough to sell if I have to."

"Forgive the question, Mom, but why this change of heart now?"

Clare grew self-conscious. "Our argument yesterday did it. I figured I'd lost you again. Then to come home and find all your things still here… The stress of the past weeks caught up with me and I completely broke down, wept with relief. Teddy found me that way and we had a long talk. He reckons that you and I are both pretty nice people who deserve to be happy, so I will never put my guilt over Brad Cutler ahead of us again. It's time for everyone to stop mourning, including the Cutlers."

"That's simply wonderful, Mom!" Kelsey kissed her cheek. "I have news, too, I'm staying on for good. I may not land a teaching job right away, or ever. But Ethan and I are committed to each other and that's a good enough beginning."

"I suppose you could join the café staff until you make solid plans," Clare offered.

"I won't push anymore. I'll come in only when you really need me."

Clare pointed at the door. "Then you better scoot over there now. Surely one Graham should be at the café at this hour."

Kelsey hadn't been on duty an hour before Ethan arrived to scoop her into his arms for an ambitious kiss, giving the patrons a floor show with their breakfast.

"You always were over the top, Ethan," Clare teased, arriving right behind him.

"This is just the entertainment you need to make this place rock," he insisted.

"Maybe you two could kiss again, say about five?" Clare teased merrily. "Just to put people in the mood for Italian?"

"My pleasure," he said, taking a seat at the counter. "So have any of you ladies talked to the Yateses today? I only ask because Derek's garage is closed, which is unusal for a Saturday."

Kelsey took the seat next to his. "Last time I spoke to them was the night before last, right after Lewis's attack. I'm afraid I totally unloaded. It's embarrassing now. No wonder they haven't returned my messages."

Linda was listening as she wiped down the granite counter. "You say Derek's garage is shut?"

Ethan nodded. "I'm sure it's nothing serious."

Linda frowned. "When I talked to Sarah last night, she wasn't her usually bouncy self. Come to think of it, she got rid of me real fast. Maybe I should drop over there. If you can manage, Kelsey?"

Kelsey waved her on.

"I can run over with you, Linda," Ethan offered.

"No," Kelsey protested. "They deserve some space from our problems. When Sarah wants us, she'll let us know."

DEREK PEERED OUT THE PICTURE window as someone pounded on the front door. "It's Ma. What'll we do, Sare?"

Sarah sighed from the hallway, sinking her teeth into an apple. "Like we have a choice. She's got a key and the nerve of Napoleon."

Seconds later the lock clicked and the door swung open to a candy-striped missile. "What is going on in here!"

"Taking a timeout from the world, is all," Derek said, firmly closing the door behind her.

"You've never closed the garage on a Saturday. You sick?"

"Ah, Ma," he moaned as Linda checked his forehead for fever.

"You need to avoid the baby if you are. I can stay to help."

"And tell Clare what?"

"It's okay. Kelsey is standing in for me. In fact, she's staying on for good. She's been calling to tell you. You should answer, be happy for her."

"Ma," Derek thundered, "quit telling us what to do!"

Linda folded her arms. "Huh. As if I could ever stop."

Sarah soberly measured Derek. "So Kelsey is staying. Time to set the record straight. Why not practice on your mother?"

"DEREK'S FEELING LOW so Linda's not coming back today," Clare announced as she hung up the wall phone behind the counter. "I can tell she's deeply upset about something."

"This might be tricky, as I was going to help Artie

create a new veggie lasagna," Kelsey said. "Guess I can pop in and out to help cover her tables."

Ethan brightened. "If you're looking for basic part-time help, I know a boy who needs spare money for car repairs."

"Ronny," Kelsey guessed.

"Right. Derek did have to put in that water pump and the boy's on a payment plan."

"Hurray for rolling money pits," Clare declared. "I'll call their house. He could start today if he likes."

"Just don't let him talk you into hiring his Stella as a waitress," Ethan cautioned. "They won't get a darn thing done between smooches."

"There's the pot calling the kettle black," Clare cracked.

Ethan slipped off his swivel chair with a chuckle. "Catch you girls later."

KELSEY AND ETHAN WERE EMERGING from the movie theater that evening when Sarah called Ethan on his cell to ask them over. Sarah answered their knock, paler and more distraught than Kelsey had ever seen her.

"What's the matter?" Kelsey asked, grasping her friend's shoulders.

Sarah shuddered a little. "Just come in."

They were herded into the dimly lit living room. It was strangely quiet, the TV screen black, the stereo quiet.

"Where are Derek and the baby?" Ethan asked.

Sarah looked disoriented. "Derek's coming. He—"

There was a pounding on the basement stairs and Derek emerged through the door. Kelsey muffled a gasp. He looked wretched and red-eyed. She'd only seen him this way when his father had been alive. What could be wrong?

"Sit down, you two," Sarah urged, pointing to the sofa.

Kelsey exchanged a worried look with Ethan but they sat.

Derek stalked closer, raking hands through his shaggy black hair. "My God. I don't know where to start."

Sarah gritted her teeth. "Just do it."

"Okay." Derek inhaled. "Kelsey. About the Cutler—"

"Stop! If this is some speech on Lewis's behalf, don't bother!"

"No, Kel," Derek cut in. "Let me talk. It's about—about prom night," he stuttered. "I know what really happened."

"You?" Ethan challenged. "You didn't even go to the prom."

"Please shut up!" Derek cried, clutching his temples. "Nothing happened the way people think. I didn't just find the accident, I was part of it. In a way, I caused it. Unintentionally."

Ethan's eyes hardened. "What are you talking about?"

Derek began to pace feverishly, as if recharging his memory, his courage. "The part about me riding around on my motorbike that night is true. But I came upon Brad's Jetta earlier on around eleven—at Shell Lake." He gazed down at Kelsey. "You were there with Brad, Todd and Lissa."

"I simply don't remember," Kelsey said resignedly.

"It was pretty dark with only a sliver of moon. But I could make out Todd and Lissa playing near the water. You and Brad were tussling on a blanket on the grassy slope." Derek stared up at the ceiling. "Brad, uh, had your dress half-off."

Kelsey put her hand to her mouth but said nothing.

"It was a bad scene, a Styrofoam cooler full of ice and beer, an open condom box, Brad with his shirt and pants undone. You and Brad were in a heated battle over sex. It looked like you'd been resisting him for a while. When I intervened, Brad became so mad he dumped the contents of the cooler over you. You screamed then shot to your feet. You were devastated, humiliated." He took a ragged breath.

"I was furious. I helped you fix your dress. That's when he lunged at us, insisted you needed to be taught a lesson about the Cutlers always getting their way. He ordered me off. Well, I was leaving all right—and taking you along. You wanted to come, lashed out to Brad that it was over between you. He flipped. It was almost funny watching the rich boy struggling with his pants and shouting to the others to help him. By the time we were on my bike, strapping on the helmets, they were stowing the blanket and cooler in the Jetta's trunk and Brad was yanking open the driver's door as we sped off.

"You begged me not to take you home, Kel, fearing that Brad would find us there and start a row with Clare. I figured we could hide out in the country for a while. Brad would soon get fed up or pass out or be distracted. Unfortunately, Brad caught up with us fast. I hadn't expected that, or the sudden rain. Suddenly we were in a chase along that slick rural road. He had the brights on us and was laying on the horn. I've always been real tough, but it was terrifying. We ended up skidding out. We both slid off the bike, Kel, and it slewed away.

Drunken Brad must've come up on my lone headlight beam, lying still and low. Likely confused, he swerved and slammed into the tree. I was okay so I took off your helmet—thank God you were wearing one—to check out your injuries. You were dazed, banged up, but you seemed coherent.

"Then I dashed to the car. It was horrific. Doors gaping open, all of them tossed out like rag dolls."

"So Brad was near the driver's door alone," Ethan sought to verify.

"That's right. He was the driver no doubt about that."

"So Kelsey must have crawled over to him, rather than the other way round."

"Yes, Ethan."

"She did that in the driving rain, despite her own injuries."

Ethan's voice was full of awe. But Kelsey couldn't connect with him, with any of them. She was paralyzed in shock.

"I wanted to take you with me, Kel, but I didn't think you'd be able to balance on the bike. So I took off alone, roared over to fetch Lewis. He called Norton, who called for rescue. I rode with Lewis in his car and we all got back to the scene about the same time. I was planning to tell the cops everything, Kel. Then suddenly Lewis was doing my talking, explaining how I'd happened on the accident. I'd actually told him that when he answered the door, just to speed things up.

"Suddenly, I was in the way. Somebody drove me back to the estate to pick up my bike. I rode on home and lay awake all night in a sweat, waiting for someone at the hospital to spill the real story, waiting to be arrested on some charge. But those three kids died. And you couldn't remember a thing.

"I intended to tell Norton. But he always had it in for me and I could only imagine how he'd twist this mess. And Lewis…I remembered how angry he was the time my mom broke a vase in his house. Now I'd actually killed his son!

"Then the craziest thing happened. Lewis wanted to reward me for my heroics. Because of me, he had a chance to say goodbye to Brad. He babbled on about boosting my image, my whole life. I thought he was just delirious with grief, so I went along. Never in my wildest nightmares, Kelsey, did I expect you to be blamed. I figured they'd put you in the passenger seat of the car, even if your position was a little off. But out of kindness you must've crawled so far, you were closer to the driver's door than Brad himself!

"Things spun out of control after that. They pounced, pressured you for answers you couldn't supply. I kept hoping it would end. But Lewis could never get enough, like his son. You were going to pay, because somebody had to. I know I should have stepped forward. But I was so scared. We Yateses were already town scum because of my dad. I believed they might have killed me somehow if I confessed. So I let you fall, Kelsey.

"Once you went away it got easier. Lewis meanwhile, had started his PR campaign on my behalf, talking me up, finding me nice rooms in town, arranging my purchase of Mel Trumbell's garage. Then Sarah came along and finally I'm living a dream life. By then you seemed content on your own. Your reports to Sarah sounded happy."

Derek began to sob and dropped to one knee before Kelsey. "I am so sorry."

Her voice was just a croak. "We were like family, a brother and sister with two moms."

"Yes. I know! Seeing you again, not especially happy after all, has brought it all back. I knew that somehow, I finally had to tell you."

"You sure were in no hurry, Derek, in spite of my struggles."

He clasped her hand in his. "I tried to hint I had something to tell you the other night at the Tick-Tock, then you started in about a lover who lied about being married, how much you hate liars. That shut me up again. Then on top of everything, Ethan decided to re-open the case! I had no idea what he might uncover. I could hardly think straight."

Ethan pinned a hard look on Derek. "Did you happen to tell Lewis about Kelsey's plans for the café? Her application for a bank loan?"

Derek gulped. "Not on purpose." Above their groans, he said, "Somebody must've told him we were all holed up in the café after closing, because around seven-thirty the next morning he was at the garage pestering me about it. You know how it is when he corners you, Ethan. I finally gave in and told him. I didn't think he'd actually stop the loan."

"Oh, Derek," Sarah huffed in disgust. "You didn't tell me that."

Kelsey appealed to Sarah now. "Did you know about the accident? All along, I mean."

Sarah was startled. "Of course not, Kel. Derek told me the night of Lewis's heart attack. Your crying in his arms did him in. We've been hiding out since then. But,

Linda made him tell her what was wrong and now she thinks her life with Clare is over. That won't happen, will it, Kel?"

Kelsey gaped, blank. "I don't know...."

"Lewis will have to be told everything, of course," Sarah said. "We understand. And volunteer for the job."

"No," Ethan said curtly. "I will run with this from here, choose the right time."

"But I should be there, too!" Derek protested frantically. "To explain, protect myself somehow. Our whole life is tied up in this."

"This is bigger than you, Derek. Far more complicated."

Derek was stunned. "Have you found out something more?"

Ethan shrugged. "That's all I care to say for now. Except to put a gag order on you two and Linda. Nobody talks about this any further until I say."

Sarah looked panicked. "So we're to simply trust you with our future?"

"After ten years of silence looking after his own interests, Derek owes Kelsey the chance to defend hers. And when I'm done," he scolded, "Kelsey will get the honor of telling Lewis what happened. She deserves it."

Derek was still kneeling, squeezing Kelsey's hand. "Will we be okay?"

"I need some space to process this," she whispered. "But nobody understands the importance of forgiveness better than I. So, yes, we'll be okay."

Pulling her forward, he kissed her cheek. "Thank you."

Kelsey wanted to park by the lake for a while, so Ethan took her there. Sitting in the front seat of the squad car, she cried softly on his shoulder for a good long while. Finally, they emerged to sit on the top of a nearby picnic table, enjoy the cool night breeze, the lap of the lake.

Sniffing, she dabbed her face with a tissue. "That whole blowup happened right here. And I never had a clue."

"The mind is a fragile thing, Kel."

"So are relationships. I sure understand Derek a lot better now. No wonder he's been acting so funny since my return."

"And now I've figured out his covetous behavior toward Lewis. He invested so much in that relationship, to the point of sacrificing you. He'd be frantic to make it work. You sure handled him like a trooper tonight. Better than he deserved."

"He's been as strong as he could be, I guess. He must have been like a starving kid in a candy store when Lewis first offered him a bright future. A huge temptation like that gives a person a split second to decide, but they have to live forever with the result." Her voice was shaky, and sure enough, Ethan had caught on to her double meaning.

"You must be just as shocked over Brad's behavior."

"I certainly am. He sometimes got impatient, but never ugly. Could be though, that through some miscommunication, he expected prom night to be payday."

"I hope you don't blame yourself for what he did."

"A lot of kids do set a date to lose their virginity at the prom. I did talk a lot about it being a big night. He must've jumped to the wrong conclusion. In any case, it'll always be painful to imagine him being so harsh. He usually treated me so well."

"I don't like to think of my buddy that way either," Ethan admitted quietly.

She patted his thigh. "We'll get beyond it, like we have everything else."

He stared out over the water. "Yes."

"What did you mean tonight when you swore the Yateses to secrecy about the accident? What are you up to, Ethan? After you found that awful file on the crash, I figured you gave up."

"I did slow up. But funny little details have continued to crowd my mind. The way Lewis has always seemed more nervous than angry about you coming back. The way he kept probing to see if I'd uncovered an ulterior motive in your return. The way he didn't want me to dig up that case file, despite his long-term obsession with the accident. And finally, at the hospital, a nurse mentioned that his orders had been obeyed back then. What orders? His son was dead.

"Just when I thought I had enough to think about, Derek gives me more. The blanket, the cooler, the cans, all of them somehow disappeared from the crash site, along with the condom box you already mentioned. Where did it all end up?"

"Maybe here in one of those." She pointed to the trash bins.

"Oh." Ethan straightened. "But Derek saw them open the trunk."

"So what? Brad might have been taking something out."

"Kel," he rumbled, "you're working against me here."

She smiled over at him softly. "Just working toward the truth."

Chapter Fourteen

Ethan locked himself in the police station Sunday afternoon, to concentrate on the crash mystery. He had been with Kelsey, Clare and Teddy all morning, first for early church service, then for a family breakfast in the Graham home. It was there Kelsey had told her family what they'd learned from Derek about the accident. Like the Yateses, the Grahams wanted to intervene with Lewis. Not to defend the guilty Derek, but wrongly accused Kelsey. Brad's reputation was going to suffer but he was just a boy who had behaved rashly. In fact, this was all about a bunch of hotheaded kids.

Whether he liked it or not, suddenly Ethan had a posse of willing, albeit hapless, deputies. When what he needed most was a word with former sheriff, Roger Norton.

His desk phone rang sharply in the quiet. The caller ID read Norton, with a Florida area code. He scooped it up. "Hello. Thanks for getting back to me, Roger. Job's going well. But we need to talk sheriff-to-sheriff about the Cutler accident. The record on file is a joke." Ethan allowed Norton to hem and haw only so long before cutting in. "Look, it's come down to you helping me out or sinking with Lewis. Seriously. Kelsey is back in town and I intend to right this wrong. Watch it, Roger, I plan to marry the girl. Now, does the original file exist? Lewis's safe, eh? But I bet you have a copy. What do you mean—maybe! This can be done hard or easy. You overnight express it to me, I'll keep you out of it and pretend I found it in the library. But if I have to fly down there to get it, your wife and neighbors are going to get a show. Good choice. Send it today. There's mail service at the airport on Sundays. In the meantime, tell me *everything*."

THE CAFÉ WAS A TENSE hive early Monday morning with scrappy, weepy queen bees Clare and Linda making up. Kelsey acted as go-between, and encouraging them to start again with a clean slate, and reminding them things could only improve for the café.

"Once Lewis discovers I wasn't in Brad's car at the time of the crash, surely he'll back off, and the old crowds will return for a new look at this place."

"And it'll be a cinch to get the teaching job you want," Clare predicted. "I say the sooner he knows, the better."

Linda bobbed her dark head. "Go tell the old buzzard his own kid caused all this misery. It'll do him good to finally face a flaw in his own family. Show him he's no better than us ordinary people."

"Ethan wants me to wait," Kelsey insisted. "He wants all of us to keep quiet just a little while longer."

"But look what the delay's doing to us," Linda complained. "Clare's a fidgety mess. Derek's a wreck. Sarah's on the verge of explosion."

"So is Teddy," Clare confided. "I've never seen him so incensed."

Their two families were as volatile as a vat of nitro, Kelsey knew. She was also anxious to reveal the truth, ached for the opportunity to trump Lewis at his own game, and then somehow begin to heal the wound they shared.

Ethan's demand for secrecy was frustrating. He'd said he didn't want word to get out until he had all the hard facts.

But what other facts could matter so much? The little details niggling at his brain seemed silly to her. Brad was rich, often threw stuff away. A cooler wouldn't matter to him. Nor would the missing blanket. Wet from the dumped ice, it would've picked up dirt and grass. She envisioned everything being wrapped in the blanket and stowed in the nearest bin, condoms included. As for Lewis giving orders at the hospital back then, he often made unnecessary, unwelcome demands, and wouldn't have been thinking straight at the time.

They opened the café and a few regulars wandered in. Artie was among them, grumbling because the rear door was locked and paranoid about the meeting he'd seen through the window.

Kelsey again thought of ripples on the water. How one event could cause so much pain. It was high time that crash was put to rest.

She stared at the door, hoping her man would walk through with a plan of action. But the hours passed and he never showed.

Finally, by mid-afternoon, Kelsey couldn't wait anymore. She smacked her check pad on the lunch counter and untied her apron. "I'm going to head over to the Cutlers' myself."

"Without Ethan?"

"It'll be okay, Mom. I have the best of news this time and I deserve the pleasure of sharing it with them."

CAROL PARKER'S EYES POPPED to discover Kelsey on the doorstep. In her surprise, her professionalism slipped. "I never figured you'd come back here."

Bailey appeared beside her, dressed in a jade linen suit that played well with her platinum hair. Dismissing the maid, Bailey scanned Kelsey's red-and-white uniform. "We certainly didn't order Cozy Home takeout. What's your business today?"

Bellowing could be heard from inside the house, Lewis wanting to know what was happening. The ever-obedient Bailey called back in reply.

"Show her in here!"

Bailey shot Kelsey a furious look then stiffly ushered her into the study.

Kelsey found Lewis behind his desk, dressed in casual wear, papers and pen at hand. It appeared he was editing articles for the newspaper. Sun streamed in through a rear window, over his thinning white hair, his grooved face. He looked tougher today as he surveyed her above thick reading glasses.

"You are persistent, Kelsey."

"The truth is worth it, Lewis."

"Have you remembered something?" he demanded sharply.

"No. Forget about that ever happening."

"All I want to do is forget about you."

His words stung but she held her ground. "Oh no, you're not going to do that."

"This is outrageous," Bailey sputtered. "You must leave, Kelsey. Now."

Instead, Kelsey sat in a chair fronting the desk. "I have something very important to tell you." She launched into her story, or rather, Derek's account of what had happened on prom night. It was embarrassing to admit what had fueled Brad's rage, but she wasn't going to leave anything out, referring to his adolescent lust as "getting fresh" in defence to the outdated mogul.

"I will continue to remember Brad with affection," she said finally. "Boys that age often get the wrong idea." She frowned. "What matters now is that you finally know that I was never reckless enough to commandeer that car, but rather, Brad was driving. As for his culpability, it's a given the road conditions were incredibly poor and would have challenged the most experienced driver. Derek made it clear that we were only trying to escape Brad, give him time to cool off. It's tragic he chose to follow us."

The room went abruptly silent. Kelsey expected Lewis to at least crumple a bit from the weight of the truth, maybe shed a tear. What he did do was tap his pen on the surface of the desk, slanting Bailey, standing by with arms folded, a look Kelsey couldn't decipher.

Bailey spoke first and only to Lewis. "What do you make of this?"

Lewis sighed. "Rubbish." As Kelsey gasped, he turned to her. "But I'm sure it suits you to believe it and I concede this must have genuinely come from the Yateses' camp for as you know, it's easy enough for me to."

"I can see the wife making this up, Lew," Bailey mused. "Wanting her best friend back in town. Wanting everyone to accept Kelsey. While you've had a firm grip on Derek all these years, Sarah's more of a rebel, and has more leverage over him now she's produced a baby."

"Yes, my love. The ultimate leverage."

Bearing witness to the inner workings of this ponderous pair made Kelsey squirm like a bug trapped in something unpleasantly sticky. "This truly happened, Lewis," she insisted. "Derek is no wimp and Sarah would never tell such a huge lie just to help me."

"People lie all the time for their own gain," Lewis said evenly, almost sympathetically.

"No! No!" Tears now stung Kelsey's eyes. It wasn't supposed to happen this way. They were supposed to cry, care, apologize to her for a change! "The truth always matters. Take it from me, the victim of life-shattering lies."

"I can see you're sincere in your own way," Lewis went on calmly. "That you truly aren't out to do me any more harm and probably will never remember a thing about the crash. Say I back off you and your mother, even promote the café for a change. Will you just give up and go back to Philadelphia?"

She jumped to her feet. "I won't! I'll never leave Ethan. I adore him and he loves me. Don't make him choose between us, Lewis."

"Like it or not," he seethed, "you *were* behind the wheel of that car. It galls me that after all these years, you still won't accept it, carry the proper blame."

Kelsey's heart pounded in her ears. Even now, he still didn't get it. "What can I do to convince you you're wrong!" she lamented.

"Nothing." The flat masculine reply came from the study door. It was Ethan, strong and tall in full uniform, hands behind his back.

"Ethan! I'm sorry." She choked back a sob.

"Never mind." He strode up beside her, briefly squeezed her neck. "Clare told me where you were.

You had every right to come here but I should have told you what I suspected a lot sooner. I just wanted to be sure. Be fair."

Lewis glared at Ethan. "What the blazes is going on? I've been trying to call you for days."

"Working hard, Lewis."

"But what if I had another episode, son?"

"Bailey would have dialed 911," Ethan bit out. "And don't call me son. It just doesn't fit anymore."

"Huh?" Lewis sank back in his big chair, realization sheeting his face. "So you're actually dumping me for this girl."

"Not for her. No, Lewis, I'm dumping you because you're a rotten human being."

An outraged Bailey was hovering at her husband's side now, protectively touching his shoulder. "How dare you, Ethan?"

With a measure of disgust, Ethan whisked a file out from behind his back and flipped it open. "Kelsey, there is a reason the Cutlers are so determined to keep you behind the wheel of that Jetta."

She was flabbergasted. "Why? What purpose would it serve?"

He gazed down at her sadly. "The man who's always insisted he and I should harbor no secrets was concealing a big one—Brad was in no condition to be driving that night. His blood-alcohol level was twice the legal limit."

"No. Oh, no." She covered her face as if to deflect the blow. The last pieces of the confusing, decade-old puzzle were floating into place. The cans Derek saw in the dark were beer cans. While Brad had occasionally sneaked a nip of booze from the Cutler stock, he never drank heavily or in public. If Brad were drunk, it explained his foolish choices, forcing himself on her, chasing the motorcycle at high speed when he had no right to be driving at all.

"All three of them were drinking," Ethan went on, as if reading her thoughts. "I can only imagine how awkward and nervous that made you feel. How anxious you must have been to leave with Derek. Escape that ugly scene."

"This is cruel hearsay!" Bailey snapped. She reached over the desk for the file. Surprising her, Ethan gladly let go of it. "It says Lissa and Todd also tested double the legal limit," she said, scanning the paperwork. "And Kelsey was cleared for alcohol. Where did this report come from, Ethan?"

"It is the official police report filed by Roger Norton at the time. Don't act as though you've never seen it, Bailey. Leave me a smidgen of respect for you."

Bailey limply dropped the heavy bound file on the desk like a bundle of trash. "It must be a forgery."

Lewis stonily eyed Ethan. "So you went digging after I told you not to. Where'd you find it? The library basement? I always worried that somebody would get hold of Roger's copy and stow it with the rest. Considering the amount of cash I laid on him, he should've burned it before he left."

"Lewis, what are you saying?" Bailey asked in an uncharacteristic whine.

Lewis spared his wife a glance. "It's best you leave us now."

"Leave you!" she repeated in disbelief.

"I'd prefer it, yes," he said more sharply.

"Prefer it all you like. Brad was my son, too. I need to know everything." Hands on hips, Bailey gazed over the desk to Ethan. "Tell me about this file. What it has to do with Lewis."

"You really don't know."

Bailey grew taut and pale. "No."

"Presumably Kelsey filled you in on the events at Shell Lake. Her fight with Brad over sex, Derek's appearance, Brad's rage at the both of them, the fatal chase." Ethan paused to frown at Bailey. "Don't work your mouth at me like you do to Lew when you're mad. You asked for the truth."

"I soft-pedaled Brad's anger," Kelsey said. "Called it *disappointment*."

"No, Bailey, this whole story has been carried along on a powerful wave of rage and self-interest, funneled first through Brad, then Lewis. Your husband arrived at the scene of the crash to discover an open trunk full of incriminating stuff—a wet messy blanket, cans of beer, an open box of condoms, a foam cooler. Any fool could see there'd been some sort of illegal, if not salacious, party. Taking charge of the scene, he ordered the kids delivered not to the nearest trauma center, but modest Maple County Hospital, where he'd have some pull in getting—and squashing—test results.

"I just got back from the hospital, by the way, where I verified everything in Norton's original report. As I had come to suspect, Lewis was quickly filled in on the blood tests. Discovering Kelsey was the only sober one, and presumably the driver, he had the tests run three times in an effort to make sense of the crash, put her in the driver's seat. When he couldn't, he sought a cover-up on the drinking angle altogether. After all, Kelsey would hardly look the master of disaster being the only sober one. Even Lewis would have had trouble selling that fiction around town."

"I didn't cover it up to punish Kelsey!" Lewis thundered. "I only wanted to protect Brad's reputation."

"That may be, Lewis, but you also didn't want to risk a whiff of liability. Which for sure would have happened if Brad had been deemed responsible for those lost lives."

"I helped those two grieving families. Showered them with cash and favors."

"And you punished the third family," Ethan said. "Left the Grahams hanging by a thread in this town, saddled them with a guilt they didn't deserve."

"But I've always believed Kelsey was driving. Honestly. I still believe it. Her purse was wedged in the seat."

"Then why have you been so worried about her motives?" Ethan demanded. "If not because you feared she remembered *Brad* being in the driver's seat?"

"I worried she had come to remember other details— specifically the drinking. How sweet it would be for her to spring that on me after all this time. You see, I couldn't believe she'd return without something to throw back at me. I've been frantic over her moves. You can understand my position. I would have been in trouble for tampering with the scene. My reputation and Brad's would both suddenly be on the line." His voice quaked at his son's name. "That would be wrong. He was the perfect child, an A student, an athlete. People still admire him. Love him." He pointed a trembling finger up at Kelsey. "You were the driver," he sobbed. "Your purse was wedged in the seat. Brad loved you so much he even crawled around the car to be near you. Wasted his last breath on you."

Ethan shook his head. "Didn't Kelsey tell you, Lew? Derek confirmed that *she* did the crawling, from where she skidded off the bike. All Brad did was fall out of the car."

"Liar!" Lewis pounded a fist on the desk. "Get out! Liars, get out!"

Ethan picked up the file and took Kelsey by the arm. Bailey stepped into their path, her blue eyes wet and vacant. "Wait. Plainly, this is the truth. Brad was our wonderful son, but he was indeed spoiled and willful. I want to apologize. Especially to you, Kelsey. You've been through a remarkable hell, you and your mother. You can tell her I will be apologizing to her as well. In person. Soon. And I will begin to make amends in any way I can. Sincerely."

"Bailey!" Lewis wailed. "Wait."

Already on her way to the door, she didn't as much as break her stride. Ethan and Kelsey followed, never looking back.

Chapter Fifteen

On a bright and sunny day later that week. Kelsey
was at the town cemetery with a bouquet of wildflow-
ers. Talking to her old boyfriend. Finally saying a
proper farewell, in full knowledge of what had
occurred and why.

The headstone was massive, of course, three feet
high, ornately sculpted with doves and crosses, etched
with a moving tribute worthy of a statesman. Washed
clean from last night's rains.

Such a big image for a young boy to live up to.

Just a boy, Kelsey reflected. Who paid the ultimate
price for dipping into adult pleasures he couldn't yet
handle.

So immersed in her thoughts, she didn't hear the approaching footsteps. But suddenly she got a whiff of a
familiar pungent hair cream that should have been
banned long ago by the Food and Drug Administration.

"Hello, Kelsey."

"Lewis," she blurted in sharp surprise. The wind
seemed stronger now as it whipped at his hair, rippled
his suit, threatened to send his stick figure sailing. "I
suppose you come here often."

"Yes. To meditate and remember." He paused, as if doing so now.

"You could have waited until I left," she chided.

"No. We need to talk and it's fitting we talk here."

"What do you mean?"

"We should talk with Brad between us. Like we used to."

She shook her head and stared at the ground. "All we had is long gone."

"The best of what I had certainly is. But recently, I've been forced to reassess my values and my actions. Concede that I got too wrapped up in grief to appreciate the blessings that survived."

"Like loyal Bailey," Kelsey dared guess.

He chuckled wryly. "Bailey is indeed the centerpiece of my life. Something she has often pointed out this week in the strongest terms. She almost left the other day," he admitted in disbelief. "Screaming that she couldn't bear to look at me, throwing things in suitcases. I'd forgotten how hard and accurately she could throw. Needless to say, the shift of power has changed slightly at the estate. Back to our newlywed days."

Kelsey exhaled impatiently. "Do you finally accept the facts, Lewis? The things so important to me?"

"It's been a rough journey. I had an overdue talk with Derek, and he was cooperative and forthcoming."

"And he likely repeated everything *I* had to say."

"I treated your version poorly, yes. But I deserve credit for recovering, trying to sort this out! Don't I?"

"Well, I'm certainly relieved everything is finally out in the open. Any further cover-up would now be impossible."

"I wouldn't even try," he retorted. "Bailey's conditions for staying on at the estate are crystal clear. Facing reality on all levels is number one."

"No more hiding behind your own prejudices, snapping orders, bending others to join you?"

His brows jumped at her nerve. "I suppose I deserve that."

"I hate the way you've messed with my mother," she seethed. "You had her spinning with guilt for ten years over nothing. Nothing." She glared at him. "All the while, pretending you weren't responsible for jeopardizing her business."

"Believe me, I intend to apologize profusely."

Kelsey smiled tightly. "I look forward to it. For my part, I will always regret not taking away Brad's car keys. Seems only fair to admit it for closure's sake. Nobody's getting out of this scot-free."

He awkwardly patted her shoulder. "You were probably too frightened to attempt it, even if you thought of it. Besides, we're not sure you didn't take them. The key I took out of the ignition that night was the spare he kept hidden under the back fender."

"His key ring was never found?"

"No. Never." He stared at the ground. "All these years I thought you grabbed the spare set and took over the wheel by force, because of the drinking. I couldn't help myself, it fit into my theory so well. So you are staying on with us for certain," he ventured, glancing up.

"That's right. I had such a happy childhood here. I hope to recapture some of that joy again with Ethan at my side."

"I will also be at your side," Lewis announced. From out of his suit jacket he pulled a folded section of newspaper. Unwrapping it, he showed her tomorrow's headline. NEW TWISTS REVEALED IN LOCAL ACCIDENT.

"Who wrote it?" Kelsey asked dubiously.

"Rebecca Burnett gets the byline. But it was a collaboration between me, Bailey and Derek, working with my copy of the real police report. I assure you all the angles are covered. There's also an interview in the same edition with Mrs. Brown about her retirement, the vacancy it will leave in the second grade. She mentions you by name, gives you her highest recommendation." He refolded the paper and handed it to her. "You are really free to make a new start, Kelsey. People will again see you for the angel you are." He blinked, his pale eyes rimmed in red. "Bradley knew what he was doing when he chose you, and I knew what I was doing when I applauded his choice. Let's move forward on that positive note."

"And forgive everyone everything?" Kelsey challenged.

"Yes, Kelsey," he huffed, "we all have suffered enough."

Kelsey bent over to stuff her bouquet in one of the rain-filled metal vases anchored in the ground. It was then she noticed Ethan standing nearby in the damp grass, protecting her back the way he had since she'd stepped off the bus. He moved up to embrace her from behind, wrap his strong arms around her shoulders and press her close.

Lewis rocked on his heels, looking rather nervous. "So, are you speaking to me yet, Ethan?"

Ethan stared into the bright blue sky. "I think I'll peruse that article first."

"Dammit, I can't do more!"

"There's always more to do, Lew. For starters, you can throttle back on giving so many orders."

"I intend to."

"You can give Clare your personal endorsement all around town, try out her new Italian dinner real soon. Better yet, bring your friends!"

"Fine. In return you'll work to forgive me," he bartered. "I can't afford to lose another son."

Ethan kissed the top of Kelsey's head. "Well, Kelsey here tells me it's necessary to forgive. Long-victimized by the unforgiving sort of makes her an expert on the subject. So I guess we're all going to try to live in peace together. You, me and my girl."

"Calling a grown woman a *girl* sounds ridiculous! Especially a capable one like Kelsey."

"What should I call her?"

Lewis scowled, appearing self-conscious. "If you went ahead and proposed, you could call her your fiancée, then eventually, your wife."

"Now, Lew, I thought you were backing off on the orders."

"Just how long were you eavesdropping on our private conversation?"

"Oh, it's all over town that Bailey pinned your ears back. That you're going to do everything you can to support Clare. You forget, gossip moves so fast in this place, we hardly need your newspaper." Sliding one arm off Kelsey, he tugged her along. "See you around, Lew."

Anxious to leave the wet, maudlin cemetery, Kelsey kept in step with him.

"Clare told me you were saying goodbye to Brad," he admitted. "Was it okay I showed up?"

"Of course. I just hope you don't think I was being silly coming here."

"I know I should be able to get past my insecurities, but will you ever truly be over Brad, the dream life he promised you?"

"That ideal future only existed in a young girl's mind. We've now had a good look at the Cutler males under pressure and it isn't a pretty sight. I suspect even if Brad had chosen to respect my wishes that night and avoided the accident, we wouldn't have lasted the year. There would have been other drinking parties at UW, other passes to dodge. Other girls handy on campus, willing to give in to him. I can assure you, I will never again wonder what could have been. What should be is more important. You and me."

Stopping on the street, Ethan seized Kelsey and, with a groan of pleasure, kissed her deeply. "I could officially propose right here and now."

She tipped teasing eyes to his. "Or you could toss in a proper meal, take me dancing in my Beauty gown. Make a real production out of it."

He beamed. "Guess I do have a reputation for productions. So what do you want to do on our first new day of freedom?"

She took a deep breath and considered it. "I think I want to settle in on a quiet park bench and finally have a look at that note you sent me."

He swallowed. "Can I be along?"

She tenderly touched his face. "Oh, yes, Ethan. I want you to read it."

* * * * *

Happily ever after is just the beginning...

Turn the page for a sneak preview of
A HEARTBEAT AWAY
by
Eleanor Jones

Harlequin Everlasting—Every great love
has a story to tell. ™
A brand-new series from Harlequin Books

S pecial? A prickle ran down my neck and my heart started to beat in my ears. Was today really special?

"Tuck in," he ordered.

I turned my attention to the feast that he had spread out on the ground. Thick, home-cooked-ham sandwiches, sausage rolls fresh from the oven and a huge variety of mouthwatering scones and pastries. Hunger pangs took over, and I closed my eyes and bit into soft homemade bread.

When we were finally finished, I lay back against the bluebells with a groan, clutching my stomach.

Daniel laughed. "Your eyes are bigger than your stomach," he told me.

I leaned across to deliver a punch to his arm, but he rolled away, and when my fist met fresh air I collapsed in a fit of giggles before relaxing on my back and staring up into the flawless blue sky. We lay like that for quite a while, Daniel and I, side by side in companionable silence, until he stretched out his hand in an arc that encompassed the whole area.

"Don't you think that this is the most beautiful place in the entire world?"

His voice held a passion that echoed my own feelings, and I rose onto my elbow and picked a buttercup to hide the emotion that clogged my throat.

"Roll over onto your back," I urged, prodding him with my forefinger. He obliged with a broad grin, and I reached across to place the yellow flower beneath his chin.

"Now, let us see if you like butter."

When a yellow light shone on the tanned skin below his jaw, I laughed.

"There...you do."

For an instant our eyes met, and I had the strangest sense that I was drowning in those honey-brown depths. The scent of bluebells engulfed me. A roaring filled my ears, and then, unexpectedly, in one smooth movement Daniel rolled me onto my back and plucked a buttercup of his own.

"And do *you* like butter, Lucy McTavish?" he asked. When he placed the flower against my skin, time stood still.

His long lean body was suspended over mine, pinning me against the grass. Daniel...dear, comfortable, familiar Daniel was suddenly bringing out in me the strangest sensations.

"Do you, Lucy McTavish?" he asked again, his voice low and vibrant.

My eyes flickered toward his, the whisper of a sigh

escaped my lips and although a strange lethargy had crept into my limbs, I somehow felt as if all my nerve endings were on fire. He felt it, too—I could see it in his warm brown eyes. And when he lowered his face to mine, it seemed to me the most natural thing in the world.

None of the kisses I had ever experienced could have even begun to prepare me for the feel of Daniel's lips on mine. My entire body floated on a tide of ecstasy that shut out everything but his soft, warm mouth, and I knew that this was what I had been waiting for the whole of my life.

"Oh, Lucy." He pulled away to look into my eyes. "Why haven't we done this before?"

Holding his gaze, I gently touched his cheek, then I curled my fingers through the short thick hair at the base of his skull, overwhelmed by the longing to drown again in the sensations that flooded our bodies. And when his long tanned fingers crept across my tingling skin, I knew I could deny him nothing.

* * * * *

Be sure to look for A HEARTBEAT AWAY,
available February 27, 2007.

And look, too, for THE DEPTH OF LOVE
by Margot Early,
the story of a couple who must learn
that love comes in many guises—
and in the end it's the only thing that counts.

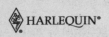

HARLEQUIN®

E V E R L A S T I N G   L O V E ™

Every great love has a story to tell ™

Fall from Grace

Kristi Gold

Save $1.⁰⁰ off

the purchase of
any Harlequin
Everlasting Love novel

Coupon valid from January 1, 2007
until April 30, 2007.

**Valid at retail outlets in Canada only.
Limit one coupon per customer.**

52607370

HECDNCPN0407

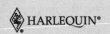

EVERLASTING LOVE™

Every great love has a story to tell™

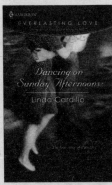

Save $1.⁰⁰ off

the purchase of any Harlequin Everlasting Love novel

Coupon valid from January 1, 2007 until April 30, 2007.

Valid at retail outlets in the U.S. only. Limit one coupon per customer.

5 65373 00076 2   (8100) 0 11302

HEUSCPN0407

REQUEST YOUR FREE BOOKS!

2 FREE NOVELS PLUS 2
FREE GIFTS!

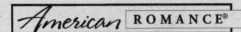

Heart, Home & Happiness!

YES! Please send me 2 FREE Harlequin American Romance® novels and my 2 FREE gifts. After receiving them, if I don't wish to receive any more books, I can return the shipping statement marked "cancel." If I don't cancel, I will receive 4 brand-new novels every month and be billed just $4.24 per book in the U.S., or $4.99 per book in Canada, plus 25¢ shipping and handling per book and applicable taxes, if any*. That's a savings of close to 15% off the cover price! I understand that accepting the 2 free books and gifts places me under no obligation to buy anything. I can always return a shipment and cancel at any time. Even if I never buy another book from Harlequin, the two free books and gifts are mine to keep forever.

154 HDN EEZK   354 HDN EEZV

Name	(PLEASE PRINT)	
Address		Apt. #
City	State/Prov.	Zip/Postal Code

Signature (if under 18, a parent or guardian must sign)

Mail to the **Harlequin Reader Service®**:
IN U.S.A.: P.O. Box 1867, Buffalo, NY 14240-1867
IN CANADA: P.O. Box 609, Fort Erie, Ontario L2A 5X3

Not valid to current Harlequin American Romance subscribers.

Want to try two free books from another line?
Call 1-800-873-8635 or visit www.morefreebooks.com.

* Terms and prices subject to change without notice. NY residents add applicable sales tax. Canadian residents will be charged applicable provincial taxes and GST. This offer is limited to one order per household. All orders subject to approval. Credit or debit balances in a customer's account(s) may be offset by any other outstanding balance owed by or to the customer. Please allow 4 to 6 weeks for delivery.

Your Privacy: Harlequin is committed to protecting your privacy. Our Privacy Policy is available online at www.eHarlequin.com or upon request from the Reader Service. From time to time we make our lists of customers available to reputable firms who may have a product or service of interest to you. If you would prefer we not share your name and address, please check here. ☐

HAR07

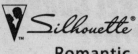

Silhouette®

Romantic
SUSPENSE

Excitement, danger and passion guaranteed!

Same great authors and riveting editorial
you've come to know and love
from Silhouette Intimate Moments.

New York Times
bestselling author
Beverly Barton
is back with the
latest installment
in her popular
miniseries,
The Protectors.
HIS ONLY
OBSESSION
is available
next month from
Silhouette®
Romantic Suspense

Look for it wherever you buy books!

Visit Silhouette Books at www.eHarlequin.com   SRSBB27525

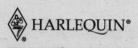

HARLEQUIN®

American ROMANCE®

COMING NEXT MONTH

#1153 HER SECRET SONS by Tina Leonard
The Tulips Saloon

Pepper Forrester has a secret—make that two secrets. Thirteen years ago she became pregnant with Luke McGarrett's twin boys and, knowing him as she did, didn't tell him he was a father. With both of them living in Tulips again, the time has come to confess. All looks to be well, until history begins to repeat itself....

#1154 AN HONORABLE MAN by Kara Lennox
Firehouse 59

Priscilla Garner doesn't want a man, nor does she need one. She's more interested in being accepted as the only female firefighter at Station 59. But when she needs a date—platonic, of course—for her cousin's wedding, she turns to one-time fling Roark Epperson. He knows she's not looking for long-term, but that doesn't mean he isn't planning on changing her mind!

#1155 SOMEWHERE DOWN IN TEXAS by Ann DeFee

Marci Hamilton loves her hometown of Port Serenity, but life's been a little dull lately. So she enters a barbecue sauce cook-off with events held all over Texas. Although it's sponsored by country music superstar J. W. Watson, Marci wouldn't recognize him—or any singer other than Willie Nelson. So when a handsome cowboy comes to her aid, she has no idea it's J.W. himself....

#1156 A SMALL-TOWN GIRL by Shelley Galloway

Still stung from her former partner's rejection, Genevieve Slate joins the police department in sleepy Lane's End hoping for a fresh start and a slower pace of life. But a sexy math teacher named Cary Hudson, a couple of crazed beagles and a town beset by basketball fever mean there's no rest in store for this small-town cop!

www.eHarlequin.com

HARCNM0207